Venetian Nights of Desire

ELLA SPENCER

DIKENGA BOOKS

Cover Design: Clarence Michael

Special discounts are available on quantity purchases.
Contact the publisher office@dikenga.com for details.

Dikenga Films | Books | Audio
www.dikenga.com

ISBN: 979-8-9910514-3-9

Venetian Nights of Desire

For the lovers.

Chapter 1

A golden haze wrapped the room, casting a tender light that seemed almost ethereal. Michael, fair-skinned with light brown hair and striking blue eyes, stood bathed in this luminous embrace, feeling the warmth and promise of an unfading love. He took a deep breath, allowing the golden light to seep into his very being, soothing the wounds left by his past.

Before him stood Gabriel, another soul treading the same celestial plane. Gabriel's eyes held an ancient knowledge of ardor, flickering like silver fish in a moonlit pool. His presence was both comforting and electrifying, a beacon of hope in Michael's turbulent sea of emotions.

In that moment of recognition, their lips, quivering with anticipation, were drawn together by an undeniable force. The kiss was a rapturous touch of lips and sighs, a dance unto itself. Every brush of their lips sent shivers down Michael's spine, each sigh a whisper of unspoken promises. Their tongues, silken ambassadors of yearning, met and intertwined, weaving their souls together. The room seemed to lean in, witnessing their union, the walls themselves holding their breath.

Gabriel's hands glided up Michael's spine, charting his lover's eagerness like a cartographer of desire. Each touch was deliberate, exploring every inch of Michael's back, memorizing the landscape of his skin. Michael reciprocated, feeling the warmth and life of Gabriel beneath his fingers. He traced the contours of Gabriel's muscles, the rise and fall of his breath, as if by touching him, he deciphered the true language of the heart.

The gossamer distance between them grew fainter, their breaths intermingling in a rhythm, like two dandelion seeds carried on the same gust of wind. Their bodies moved closer, drawn together by an invisible thread of longing and connection. The scent of Gabriel's skin, a mix of earth and musk, filled Michael's senses, grounding him in the present moment.

But unease began to claw at the corners of Michael's consciousness. A shadow of doubt crept in, whispering that this dream could not last. The threads of light coiled tighter around them, and what had once been a sensual embrace started to smother, leaving him gasping for air. He struggled to hold on to the moment, to the feeling of Gabriel's touch, but the darkness crept closer.

Gabriel's face, once the visage of passion and love, twisted into a darkened mask of anguish. His eyes, which had sparkled with the light of a thousand stars, now seemed hollow and distant. The kiss, a revelation of tender yearning, transformed into something ravenous, consuming Michael's very essence as though it were a soul-sucking beast. Each kiss, each touch, became a desperate grasp, a plea for salvation that neither could grant.

Panic erupted like a volcano, its boiling chaos wrenching Michael from the dream. He bolted awake, sitting upright in his bed, his heart galloping. The remnants of the golden haze still lingered in his mind as the warmth and light faded, leaving him alone in the cold reality of his Los Angeles apartment. The regular morning light bathed the room, a stark contrast to the vivid dream that had just unraveled. The transition from dream to reality was jarring, leaving him disoriented and breathless.

He turned his head, his heart jolting with fear as he saw his ex-partner, Bernie, lying in bed beside him. Bernie's eyes gleamed with an unsettling intensity, a chilling contrast to the warmth Michael had just felt in his dream.

"Good morning," Bernie said in a chillingly calm voice, his smile devoid of any genuine emotion.

Michael's voice trembled, his face pale as he stammered, "What are you doing here?"

Bernie's expression darkened, becoming menacing. "I thought we could give it another shot, you know, get back together."

Michael's terror rose, his body tense as he shouted, "Are you out of your mind? Get out! You stole everything from me. My money, my business, my future. You destroyed me."

Bernie's sinister smile widened. "Oh, that's all water under the bridge."

Before Michael could react, Bernie's face contorted, transforming into something grotesque and animalistic. His teeth elongated into razor-sharp fangs, saliva dripping from the corners of his mouth as he snarled. With the speed of a predator, he lunged towards Michael.

"You're a monster! Get away from me! Don't do this!" Michael cried tearfully, his voice cracking with desperation.

He scrambled to escape, but Bernie was relentless in

his pursuit. The room had become a nightmarish cage, the walls closing in as Michael fought for his life against the man who once claimed to love him. The air was thick with fear and desperation, each breath a struggle as Michael's world crumbled around him.

Bernie's grotesque features loomed closer, his fangs bared and ready to strike. Michael's mind raced, searching for an escape, but the nightmare held him fast. His body trembled, and he could feel his strength waning as Bernie's monstrous form bore down on him.

With a final, desperate surge of energy, Michael threw himself to the side, narrowly avoiding Bernie's snapping jaws. He stumbled towards the door, his vision blurred by tears and terror. The distance to safety seemed insurmountable, but he forced himself to move, driven by the primal need to survive.

As Michael reached for the door handle, he felt Bernie's clawed hand graze his back, tearing through his shirt and leaving a searing pain in its wake. He yanked the door open and hurled himself through the threshold, slamming it shut behind him. The door rattled as Bernie pounded against it, his snarls echoing through the apartment.

Michael's heart raced as he backed away from the door, his breath coming in ragged gasps. The reality of his situation crashed over him like a tidal wave. He was trapped in a living nightmare, and the only way out was to confront the monster that had invaded his life.

He gathered his resolve, his fear transforming into a fierce determination. He would not let Bernie's twisted form destroy him. With a deep breath, Michael steeled himself for the battle ahead, ready to face whatever horrors awaited him.

The door shuddered under Bernie's relentless assault, but Michael stood firm, his mind clear and focused. He was no longer the broken man Bernie had left behind. He was a survivor, and he would fight to reclaim his life, no matter the cost.

Michael bolted awake, for real this time. His heart pounded as he sat up, his eyes watering from the intensity of the nightmare. The regular morning light bathed the room, a stark contrast to the vivid and terrifying dream he just experienced. He reached out to the empty space in the bed next to him, feeling a wave of relief wash over him. "Phew," he muttered to himself, "thank god."

The nightmare had ended, yet it clung to his skin, a haunting reminder of the exquisite pleasure and sorrow that lived just below the surface of his consciousness. The vivid images and emotions lingered, like a dream waiting to be dreamt once more.

From his window, the sprawling skyline of Los Angeles stretched out before him, a testament to the bustling city where he lived. The sight of the city grounded him in reality, offering a sense of normalcy in the wake of his turbulent dreams.

Michael stood in his bathroom, the morning light filtering through the small window. He listened to the radio while brushing his teeth, the familiar routine providing a sense of normalcy. The sound of a guest speaking caught his attention.

"Hey there. I'm a gay man about to turn 30, which is like ancient. What advice do you have for moving on at my age?" the guest asked, his voice carrying a mix of anxiety and hope.

Michael paused, rinsing and gargling as he waited for the response. The Advice Doc's voice came through the radio, calm and reassuring. "Age doesn't mean any less value as a human being when it comes to finding love. Go out and meet new people. Don't be afraid to strike up a conversation with strangers because sometimes the best people for us are the ones we would never have thought to be with in the first place. Love is out there; you just need to be open to finding it."

Michael spat the remainder of the toothpaste into the sink, contemplating the advice. The words resonated with him, stirring a sense of possibility and a faint glimmer of hope. As he looked at his reflection in the mirror, he felt a renewed determination to face the day and whatever it might bring.

Chapter 2

Michael's apartment, a small yet cozy space, was filled with quirky artwork and an eclectic mix of furniture that reflected his unique taste. The living room was a blend of modern and vintage pieces, creating an inviting atmosphere. Soft, natural light streamed in through the large windows, highlighting the vibrant colors of the paintings on the walls.

Michael sat on the plush couch, looking much healthier than he did in the nightmares that haunted him. His muscular, six-foot-tall frame relaxed slightly as he handed a glass of wine to his best friend, Liza.

Liza, a pretty bisexual woman in her late twenties with gleaming brown eyes and a stylish flair, accepted the glass. Her smoky voice added to her fiery personality, which was evident in her witty and insightful blog posts. She took a sip of wine, her eyes never leaving Michael's face.

"How'd the date go?" she asked, her tone both curious and concerned.

Michael looked down, a sigh escaping his lips. "Frustrating. It feels like most gay guys just want to be... intimate without any actual intimacy."

Liza listened intently, her gaze softening as she

absorbed his words.

Michael continued, his exasperation evident. "It's like, sure, we can have a great time in bed, but when it comes to actually getting to know each other, there's just... nothing."

Liza nodded thoughtfully. "Not everyone is like that, Michael. There are guys out there looking for something meaningful, just like you are."

A brief silence settled between them, filled only by the ambient sounds of the city outside. Liza broke the silence, her voice gentle but probing. "Are you depressed?"

Michael sighed deeply, the weight of his emotions pressing down on him. "I don't... I don't know."

Liza's concern was palpable. "Have you considered talking to a therapist?"

"I'm not sure it would help," Michael admitted, his voice tinged with uncertainty. "I just feel so lost right now. It's like I've forgotten how to be happy. Like my inner bright light was set at 110 and now it's been replaced by a cheap LED bulb."

Liza leaned closer, her expression caring and earnest. "That's exactly why I think therapy might be helpful. They're like emotional electricians. Mine is a genius, actually. Want their info?"

Michael hesitated, his reluctance clear. "Maybe. I just... I don't know if I'm ready to open up to a stranger."

"I understand," Liza said gently. "But remember, they've likely heard it all before, even the saucy bits, and they're trained to provide a safe and supportive space for you."

With a reassuring smile, Liza pulled out her phone and shared her therapist's contact information with

Michael. He took the phone, looking at the details, feeling a glimmer of hope. The possibility of finding some clarity and peace, of rekindling his inner light, seemed a little more tangible with Liza's unwavering support.

Liza put her phone down and looked at Michael, her eyes softening with a mix of empathy and determination. "You know, Michael, when I first started seeing my therapist, I was in such a dark place. I felt like I was completely alone, like no one could understand what I was going through."

Michael looked at her, curiosity mingling with concern in his blue eyes. "Really? I had no idea."

She nodded, taking another sip of her wine. "Yeah, it was tough. I was struggling with my identity, my relationships, everything. But therapy helped me see things from a different perspective. It made me realize that I wasn't alone, that there were people who cared about me and wanted to help."

Michael listened intently, his heart warming at her vulnerability. "Liza, I had no idea you were going through that. You always seem so strong and confident."

Liza chuckled softly, a bittersweet smile playing on her lips. "We all have our battles, Michael. Sometimes the people who seem the strongest are the ones who are hurting the most. But you were there for me, even when you didn't know it. Your friendship kept me going."

Michael felt a lump form in his throat. "I'm glad I could be there for you. You've always been my rock, Liza. I don't know what I'd do without you."

Liza reached out and squeezed his hand, her touch warm and reassuring. "And I'm here for you now. Whatever you're going through, you don't have to face it alone."

Michael squeezed her hand back, his heart swelling with gratitude. "Thank you, Liza. You have no idea how much that means to me."

They sat in comfortable silence for a moment, the bond between them stronger than ever. The weight of the world seemed a little lighter, knowing they had each other.

"Love you," Liza said softly, her eyes gleaming with sincerity.

"Love you too," Michael replied, his voice filled with emotion.

The simple exchange of words carried a depth of meaning, a testament to their unwavering friendship and the unspoken support that bound them together. As they sat there, sharing a moment of connection and understanding, Michael felt a glimmer of hope. With Liza by his side, he knew he could face whatever challenges lay ahead.

Michael nervously paced the living room of his apartment, the quirky artwork and eclectic furniture a comforting backdrop as he clutched his phone. He took a deep breath, trying to steady his racing heart, and dialed a number. The phone rang, each tone heightening his anxiety until a soothing voice answered on the other end.

"Hello, Dr. Gika," the voice greeted warmly.

"Uh, hi. My name is Michael. I was referred to you by my friend, Liza, one of your—" Michael stammered, his nerves evident.

"Oh, the wondrous, extraordinary Liza. Such a beaming soul," Dr. Gika interjected, her voice filled with genuine affection.

Michael smiled faintly, feeling a bit more at ease. "Yes, she's pretty great. I'd... I'd like to make an appointment to see you for... therapy?"

"Of course, Michael. I'm here for you. What's been going on in your life that's brought you to me?" Dr. Gika asked gently.

Michael paused, hesitating as he gathered his thoughts. "Well, you see, I... My partner of 10 years turned out to be a sociopath, embezzled all of my money, and abandoned me. It's been almost a year, and I'm still struggling with it."

Dr. Gika's voice was filled with empathy and understanding. "Michael, the pain this person has caused clearly impacts you deeply. I recognize your suffering and am here to support you as we navigate your emotions, working together towards healing and growth."

Michael started to feel a sense of relief and comfort. "Thanks. I just... I feel so lost, you know? And I think it's time I faced this head-on and started healing."

"That's a brave decision, Michael. Does Tuesday at 3 pm work for you?" Dr. Gika inquired.

"Yeah, that sounds great," Michael responded, a bit of hope seeping into his voice.

"Fantastic. I'll see you then, Michael. Just remember, you're taking the first step towards healing, and that's something to be proud of," Dr. Gika affirmed.

"Thank you, Dr. Gika. I really appreciate it. See you Tuesday," Michael said, feeling a weight lift off his shoulders as he hung up.

The phone call ended, leaving Michael standing in the middle of his living room. He took another deep breath, feeling a mix of apprehension and optimism. The first step had been taken, and with Liza's support and Dr. Gika's guidance, he began to believe that healing was possible.

Chapter 3

Michael stood outside Dr. Gika's office, the building's exterior blending seamlessly with the surrounding cityscape. The office was housed in a modest yet inviting building, with a small sign displaying Dr. Gika's name and title. The entrance was framed by neatly trimmed shrubs, offering a sense of calm and order.

Michael approached the door, feeling the weight of anticipation and nervousness pressing down on him. He took a deep breath, his chest rising and falling as he tried to steady himself. The memory of his conversation with Dr. Gika echoed in his mind, giving him the courage he needed.

With a final exhale, Michael reached for the door handle, feeling the cool metal against his palm. He opened the door and stepped inside, the quiet hum of the office welcoming him into a new chapter of his journey towards healing.

Michael stepped into Dr. Gika's office, immediately enveloped by a serene and harmonious atmosphere. The room was a thoughtful blend of traditional and new age elements, designed to promote peace and healing. Soft lighting bathed the space, creating a warm and inviting glow.

Various crystals and decorations of enlightenment were thoughtfully placed around the room. An impressive amethyst geode acted as a powerful centerpiece on a small table, its deep purple hues catching the light. Polished pieces of rose quartz were scattered throughout the room, serving as gentle reminders of self-love and compassion. On one wall hung a colorful, handcrafted chakra tapestry, each vibrant color symbolizing a different aspect of spiritual balance. Nearby, a small brass Buddha statue sat serenely, exuding a sense of calm and mindfulness.

Dr. Gika, a friendly and caring presence, stood to greet Michael with a warm smile. Her aura was one of compassion and understanding, instantly putting Michael at ease.

"Hello, Michael. Welcome," Dr. Gika said, her voice soothing and melodic. "I'm glad you're here. Let's begin our journey towards healing, understanding, and most importantly—reclaiming your life."

Michael felt a surge of hope and determination as he took in the tranquil surroundings. The environment, combined with Dr. Gika's welcoming demeanor, made him feel that he was in the right place to start his healing journey.

As Dr. Gika welcomed Michael into the room, she gestured for him to sit in a comfortable chair near the amethyst geode. The rich purple stone seemed to emanate a calming energy, and Michael found himself relaxing slightly as he settled in. Dr. Gika took a seat across from him, her eyes filled with empathy and a genuine desire to help.

Dr. Gika gently shut the door, signaling the start of Michael's journey towards healing and self-discovery.

The room was bathed in the soft, warm glow of a Himalayan salt lamp, casting a soothing light across the serene space. Dr. Gika, an empathetic and skilled therapist, sat in a plush chair, attentively listening to Michael, who was fidgeting on the sofa across from her.

Michael took a deep breath, opening up with a hint of sadness in his voice. "I just feel like... like I've been living in the shadows since Bernie left. That's his name... Since he did what he did, it's like I can't trust myself to make the right decisions anymore."

Dr. Gika leaned forward, her expression supportive and understanding. "Michael, it's perfectly natural to feel that way after experiencing such a betrayal. But remember, trust is something that can be rebuilt."

Michael sighed, the weight of his emotions evident. "I know, it's just... it's so hard to let go of the fear that it'll happen again, you know? I've put up these walls, and I don't know how to break them down."

Dr. Gika smiled gently. "Michael, it's important to recognize that healing is a gradual process, and it's perfectly normal to encounter challenges along the way. Our purpose here is to collaborate and uncover strategies that will empower you to regain control and autonomy in your life."

She leaned forward slightly, her eyes filled with encouragement. "Let us begin by directing our attention to things you enjoy. What activities resonate deeply with you and enliven your spirit?"

Michael thought for a moment, his expression softening. "Well, I love traveling and photography. When I'm lost in a new city, with new sights, it feels like I'm connecting with a deeper part of myself."

Dr. Gika nodded appreciatively. "That's wonderful,

Michael."

Michael hesitated slightly, a blush creeping onto his cheeks. "There's another aspect of my life where I've found a lot of passion..."

Dr. Gika's eyes lit up with interest. "Oh? What is it?"

Michael blushed more, looking down for a moment before meeting her gaze again. "Well... You see..."

The scene shifted, transitioning into a series of vivid memories as Michael recalled the moments that had shaped his passions and identity.

Michael remembered standing in a secluded field on a bright day, the sun casting sharp shadows on the ground. He was with a man dressed in military fatigues. The scent of earth and grass filled the air, and the distant hum of the base faded away as they found a hidden spot. The soldier dropped to his knees, unzipped Michael's pants and opened his plump lips, sticking out his moist tongue. The soldier performed the act with a mechanical precision that left Michael feeling momentarily satisfied but ultimately hollow. The roughness of the fatigues and the soldier's firm grip added to the rawness of the moment, but there was no real connection, no warmth. It was a fleeting encounter that left Michael breathless from the act itself, but empty and unfulfilled inside.

Next, Michael recalled being naked in a dimly lit massage parlor, where the air was thick with the scent of essential oils, musky man scent, and soft music played in the background. He was bent over a massage table, his body tensed with anticipation. The masseur, with skilled and firm hands, moved closer to enter Michael from behind. Their bodies connected in a deeply intimate way, but the rhythm of their movements, while physically satisfying, was devoid of any real emotion. The physical connection provided Michael with a temporary escape from his thoughts, grounding him in the raw sensations of the moment. Yet, he felt both vulnerable and powerful, lost in the intensity of the experience, but it was a shallow intensity that left him feeling even more isolated afterward.

Michael then remembered being in a dimly lit apartment, the atmosphere charged with anticipation. He was with another man, their connection palpable but ultimately superficial. They exchanged glances filled with longing and desire, but it was a hollow desire. The man moved closer, and their bodies entwined in a passionate embrace that ignited a fire within Michael. Each touch, each kiss, each grinding of their bulges made him feel alive and desired, but it was a transient feeling, like a spark that quickly fades. The intimacy they shared was purely physical; it was a moment of connection that made Michael feel seen and valued in the moment, but left him feeling empty and disconnected once it was over.

Michael's mind snapped back to the present, the memories vivid and intense. He looked at Dr. Gika, his cheeks flushed with the intensity of his recollections. Taking a deep breath, his eyes met Dr. Gika's with a mixture of vulnerability and resolve. "I've been hooking up with strangers. A lot of strangers," he admitted, his voice trembling slightly.

Dr. Gika nodded, her expression non-judgmental and compassionate. "I appreciate your honesty, Michael."

"It's been a way for me to feel alive, desired, and, in a way, in control of my life," Michael continued, the words spilling out as if they had been held back for too long.

Dr. Gika leaned in slightly, her gaze steady and curious. "I'm curious to know, what do you feel during these interactions?"

Michael hesitated, his nerves evident, but he pushed through. "During, I feel a rush of excitement, passion, and connection. But afterward, if I'm being honest, I feel empty and disconnected. It's like a temporary high, and then I'm left feeling... broken."

"Your openness is appreciated, Michael. How was your sex life before?" Dr. Gika asked gently.

Michael shrugged, a hint of sadness in his eyes. "So-so. Pretty much non-existent."

Dr. Gika reached over to a nearby table and handed Michael a small journal. "I have a reflective assignment for you. Consider what you genuinely desire in a more profound, meaningful relationship."

Michael opened the journal, curiosity lighting up his face. "What do you want me to do?"

"Over the next week, I'd like you to note down the qualities and values that matter most to you in a partner and relationship," Dr. Gika explained, her tone encouraging. "Reflect on the type of connection you envision and what you believe will bring a sense of fulfillment."

Michael nodded, feeling a sense of purpose. "It's been a long time since I've really thought about what I want in a partner."

"That's perfectly fine, Michael. This task offers an opportunity to reevaluate and rediscover your desires and needs," Dr. Gika reassured him, her supportive presence a comforting balm.

Michael took a deep breath, feeling a sense of hope

and determination. With Dr. Gika's guidance, he was ready to delve deeper into his experiences and begin the process of healing and self-discovery.

Chapter 4

The room was filled with morning light, revealing an elegant yet cozy interior. The soft hues of the sun danced across the walls, casting a warm glow over the carefully selected furnishings and tasteful decorations. Michael sat on the couch, holding a cup of coffee, lost in deep thought. His mother, Lynn, a witty and wealthy divorcee in her 60s, entered the room, bringing a plate of freshly sliced banana bread. The aroma of the bread mingled with the rich scent of his coffee, creating a comforting atmosphere.

"You know what they say, eating solves every problem. Except losing weight," Lynn quipped, her voice filled with warmth and humor as she sat down next to Michael, offering him a slice.

"Thanks, Mom," Michael said, taking a bite. The bread was warm and moist, with just the right amount of sweetness. They sat in comfortable silence for a moment, the only sound being the gentle ticking of a nearby clock and the occasional chirping of birds outside the window.

Lynn broke the silence, her tone more serious. "You know, your father wasn't the first man who betrayed me."

Michael looked at her, surprise evident in his eyes.

"Really? You've never talked about that."

"Well, it's not exactly a topic I enjoy discussing. But I want you to know I've been where you are. And I came out stronger," Lynn said, her eyes reflecting years of wisdom and resilience.

"How?" Michael asked softly, genuinely curious.

Lynn smiled and took a deep breath. "My mother, your grandmother, once told me something I've never forgotten. 'We come from a long line of warriors. Cut off our feet and we'll learn how to walk.'"

Michael's eyes widened, taken aback by her words. "Wow."

"It's true, Michael. No matter what life throws at us, we always find a way to overcome it. We're survivors. And you, my son, are no exception. What that man did to you is outrageous, yes. But that doesn't define you. You're stronger than you think, Michael," Lynn said, her voice filled with conviction.

Michael soaked in her words, feeling a sense of hope and determination begin to grow within him.

"You're a warrior. And you'll find your way through this," Lynn continued, watching him closely. She reached into her stack of magazines and pulled out an issue with Venice, Italy on the cover. She handed it to him. "I love you," she said, her voice gentle and loving.

Michael looked at the magazine, confused. "What is this?"

"Just for you. It's where I went after your father left. It helped me heal in ways I can't describe," Lynn explained.

Michael was stunned. "Mom, I... this is too much. You already pay my rent."

"And I would do it again a million times. Son, it's time

for you to rediscover yourself and celebrate your new freedom," Lynn said, her tone resolute and loving.

Michael considered this, still in disbelief. "I can't accept this, Mom. It's just..."

"Nonsense. You deserve it. Plus, I'm rich. And, Bernie's been out of your life for almost a year now. I think it's time for you to move on, enjoy life, and start finding yourself again," Lynn insisted, her determination unwavering.

Michael hesitated, the weight of the decision lingering in his mind. The thought of Venice, a place of beauty and history, began to stir something within him—a sense of adventure, of possibility. Maybe this was exactly what he needed to start healing and rediscovering himself.

As they sat together, Lynn's phone buzzed on the coffee table. She glanced at it and then looked back at Michael. "You know, Venice is a city of masks and secrets, but also of art and love. It's a place where you can lose yourself and find yourself at the same time."

Michael flipped through the magazine, captivated by the stunning images of Venice's canals, *gondolas*, and historic architecture. The idea of wandering through its narrow streets and discovering its hidden treasures felt like a balm for his wounded soul. "Mom, I really appreciate this. I just don't know if I'm ready."

Lynn placed a reassuring hand on his. "You don't have to decide right now. Just think about it. Sometimes a change of scenery can do wonders for the heart and mind."

Michael nodded, feeling the warmth of her support. "I'll think about it."

They spent the rest of the morning talking, reminiscing about happier times, and sharing stories of resilience and strength. Lynn told Michael about her own journey of self-discovery after her divorce, how she traveled, met new people, and found solace in unexpected places. Her stories were filled with laughter and a few tears, but they all carried the same message of hope and renewal.

Michael listened intently, feeling more connected to his mother than he had in a long time. He realized that he wasn't alone in his struggles and that his path to healing might just be starting with this conversation.

As the day progressed, the idea of going to Venice started to feel less daunting and more like an opportunity. Michael began to see it not just as a trip, but as a chance to rebuild his life, to find new passions, and perhaps even to discover a new love.

By the time evening fell, the decision didn't seem so impossible anymore. Michael looked at his mother, gratitude filling his heart. "Thank you, Mom. For everything."

Lynn smiled, her eyes shining with love and pride. "You're welcome, Michael. Just remember, you're stronger than you think. And whatever happens, I'm here for you."

Michael felt a sense of peace he hadn't felt in a long time. He looked at the magazine cover one last time, the beautiful image of Venice reflecting a new beginning. Maybe, just maybe, this trip would be the start of something wonderful.

Chapter 5

Madame Zara's apartment was a vibrant reflection of her punk rock and burlesque persona, filled with eclectic decor and dramatic flair. The walls were adorned with bold artwork, vintage concert posters, and various trinkets from her colorful past. The aroma of a meal in preparation wafted through the air, mingling with the faint sounds of punk rock playing in the background.

Madame Zara herself, a punk rock legend and burlesque star, was busy in the kitchen. Her colorful tattoos and dramatic makeup added to her larger-than-life presence, and her outfit—a mix of punk rock edge and burlesque glam—only enhanced her unique style. She hummed along to the music, the energy in the room as lively as her personality.

Suddenly, a knock on the back door interrupted her culinary focus. With an intense scowl, she swung the door open, clearly annoyed by the unexpected visitor.

"Michael! Seriously?" she snapped, her voice filled with irritation.

Michael stood at the door, a hopeful look on his face. He was dressed casually, but there was a certain tension in his posture. "Madame Zara, I need to—"

"What the hell are you doing here? It's my freakin' day

off. What part of 'no psychic readings today' do you not understand?" she demanded, crossing her arms and tapping her foot impatiently.

Michael grinned, trying to diffuse her irritation with humor. "Well, I thought you, of all people, would've known I was coming."

Madame Zara rolled her eyes and snorted, her impatience palpable. "Oh, ha ha. Call me tomorrow to make an appointment. Now, get lost."

Ignoring her, Michael boldly walked past her into the kitchen. The room was a chaotic blend of culinary ingredients and mystical paraphernalia. Crystal balls, tarot cards, and incense sticks sat alongside pots, pans, and ingredients for her vegan lasagna. "But I really need to know what I should do about traveling alone for the first time since—"

Madame Zara clenched her jaw, clearly begrudging his persistence. She took a deep breath, her annoyance slowly giving way to a reluctant acceptance. "Alright, fine. But you're getting my off-the-clock spirits and they aren't always interested."

She let out an exhaustive sigh and stomped over to a table with a crystal ball on it, her movements dramatic and exasperated. She sat down heavily, her presence commanding the room. She looked down into the crystal ball, her face a mask of disinterest as she half-heartedly began her reading.

"Uh huh... Yeah... Casanova, Casanova, Casanova. Yeah, whatever..." she muttered sarcastically, turning away from the crystal ball with a dismissive wave. Her voice was filled with a mix of sarcasm and genuine irritation, as if she were performing a routine she'd done a thousand times but would rather not be doing at all.

"They tell me you need to ask the Wizard," she continued, clearly uninterested. "Go talk to the wizard. Not me. It's like going to the dentist when you need a haircut."

Madame Zara walked back to the door and opened it, her impatience evident. "Now, beat it! I've got a vegan lasagna in the oven, and I'm not letting it burn because of you."

Realizing he wouldn't get any more out of her today, Michael nodded and left. As he stepped out, he glanced back to see Madame Zara already returning to her kitchen, her focus shifting back to her meal. The door closed behind him with a finality that echoed Madame Zara's insistence on her personal time.

Outside, Michael took a deep breath, the cool air a stark contrast to the chaotic warmth of Madame Zara's apartment. He felt a mixture of frustration and amusement at the encounter. Despite her brusque manner, he knew Madame Zara had a good heart and always ended up giving him some form of advice, whether he liked it or not.

As he walked away, Michael couldn't help but think about her parting words. "Ask the Wizard." It was cryptic, even for her. He shook his head, a small smile forming on his lips. Madame Zara always had a way of making life feel like one big, unpredictable adventure. And maybe, just maybe, that was exactly what he needed right now.

Chapter 6

It was the kind of lethargic afternoon that wrapped itself around a lake like an unanswered question. The university campus was quiet, with only a few students lingering, their voices low and contemplative. The breeze carried the scent of blooming flowers and freshly cut grass, creating an atmosphere of peaceful introspection. Michael, perched on the edge of a weathered wooden bench, turned to face an older man, his former college professor, Andreas.

"Professor, what is it about life and love that makes it all so incomprehensible?" Michael asked, his voice tinged with the frustration of someone seeking answers in a world filled with uncertainties. His eyes, a mix of blue and gray, reflected the turmoil inside him.

The older man, distinguished by the weight of knowledge and experience, smiled with an air of understanding. His silver hair and gentle eyes reflected a lifetime of learning and teaching. He exuded a calm wisdom that seemed to radiate from within. "Ah, Michael, none of that can be grasped with your mind, but with your entire being. It's like the wind, moving around us, and through us. The wind does not discriminate or judge. It is within you, just waiting to be released."

Michael frowned slightly, trying to absorb the metaphor. "But how?" he asked, his voice a whisper of uncertainty.

The professor's eyes crinkled as he smiled. "The key is to be present, to feel without judgment or expectation. Let go of the fears and doubts that keep you from fully experiencing life. Allow yourself to be vulnerable, and in doing so, you open yourself up to the world."

Michael shifted on the bench, the weight of his thoughts pressing down on him. "I'm afraid of being hurt again," he admitted, his voice soft and vulnerable.

Andreas nodded, his expression sympathetic. "Fear, my dear boy, is a natural part of life. But when we let it control us, it keeps us from experiencing the beauty that life has to offer. Embracing life means facing those fears, and in doing so, we become stronger and more resilient. Trust in yourself and the journey you're on."

Michael's eyes narrowed, his expression tightening into something resembling a reflection cast upon rippling water. "So, it's like, true passion isn't just about what we know or understand, but about the journey, the uncharted territory that lies ahead?" he asked, a hint of determination creeping into his voice.

The professor, pleased with Michael's interpretation, leaned forward, his eyes reflecting a lifetime of exploration and discovery. "Precisely. Embracing the unknown, the limitless possibilities, grants us a taste of the sublime, a glimpse of the transcendent. It is in the pursuit of the elusive that we find not only our passion but our humanity. Love, then, becomes a journey, a quest for the ineffable, and it is in that very act of seeking that we come to know ourselves."

Andreas continued, his voice growing more intense,

"The unknown becomes an invitation, an unbridled exploration. And it is there, at the very edge of the infinite, that one must find the courage to leap, hands outstretched. And embrace it."

Michael took that in and sat with it for a moment, the weight of the words settling into his consciousness. The sun cast long shadows on the grass, the afternoon slowly turning to evening. "Have you ever had a partner?" he asked, curious about the man who seemed to have all the answers.

The professor's gaze, once fixed on the landscape, returned to Michael, and his lips curved into a wistful smile. He reclined on the bench, his fingers interlaced as if in quiet contemplation of the years gone by. "Ah, I've had many partners in my time, each one unique and beautiful in their own way," he began, his voice filled with fond memories.

The professor, his face softened by the wisdom of years, tilted his head slightly, the subtle movement suggesting a profound contemplation that seemed to reach into the very depths of his being. "And remember, love and sensuality are not only about physical pleasure. It is about understanding the very essence of another person and allowing them to see your own. It is a dance of souls, as much as it is a dance of bodies."

Michael stared into the professor's hypnotic eyes, feeling a mixture of admiration and longing. "Andreas, I really want to kiss you right now," he said, the words escaping before he could stop them.

The professor, caught in the unexpected intimacy of the moment, hesitated, his eyes searching Michael's with a mixture of surprise and cautious reflection. His voice, gentle and measured, sought to find the delicate balance between emotion and wisdom. "Michael, I am both flattered and humbled by your words. However, as your former professor, I have a certain responsibility, a duty to maintain boundaries that ensure mutual respect and trust."

His gaze, tempered with the warmth of understanding, communicated a kindness that transcended mere words. "It is important that we respect and honor the relationships that have shaped us, and seek connections that nourish our growth and understanding."

"Sorry, I didn't mean to overstep any boundaries. You must have known I was always attracted to you," Michael said, feeling a twinge of regret for his impulsiveness.

The professor, his demeanor reflecting a deep-rooted understanding and empathy, offered a reassuring smile. "Apology accepted. As a teacher, I have seen many students grapple with a myriad of emotions, including attraction. It is not uncommon, and I hold no judgment against you."

His words, woven with a delicate wisdom, emphasized the importance of respecting and acknowledging feelings without allowing them to define or dictate one's actions. "It is crucial, however, to recognize and respect the boundaries that exist within certain relationships. By doing so, we create a space that allows for growth, without compromising the foundation of trust and understanding."

"I always misunderstand anything genuine and connect it immediately to sex," Michael admitted, feeling exposed but also relieved to voice his confusion.

The professor, his expression imbued with empathy and insight, considered Michael's words carefully before responding, his voice gentle yet resolute. "Michael, merging genuine connections with sexual desire is common. Emotions are intricate and manifest in numerous ways. In a world where intimacy and vulnerability are often obscured by superficiality and surface-level interactions, it's easy to mistake the profound resonance of genuine connection for sexual attraction. Our society tends to place a strong emphasis on sexuality, which can further blur the lines between emotional intimacy and physical desire."

His eyes, steady and compassionate, offered a sense of understanding that transcended judgment. "To discern between connection and attraction, attune to your emotions and understand your feelings."

Michael absorbed his words, feeling a mixture of clarity and introspection. The professor's advice seemed to illuminate the path before him, casting light on the complexities of his emotions. "My mom gifted me a trip to Venice, Italy, and I don't know if I should go or not. I haven't traveled anywhere since the breakup."

The professor's face softened, his eyes taking on a wistful quality as he contemplated the possibility of such a journey. "Ah, Venice," he said, his voice filled with a sense of nostalgia and longing.

He paused, his gaze steady and unwavering, a spark of wisdom dancing in the depths of his eyes. "If I were in your shoes, I would embrace this opportunity with an open heart and an eager mind. The experiences that await you in Venice have the power to expand your horizons and enrich your life in ways that you may never have imagined."

Michael sat with the professor's words, feeling a shift within himself. The idea of Venice, a place of beauty and mystery, began to take root in his mind, offering a glimmer of hope and a promise of new beginnings. The sun continued its descent, casting a golden hue over the campus, and Michael felt a sense of peace settling over him.

"Andreas, thank you. Your words have given me a lot to think about," Michael said, his voice filled with gratitude.

The professor smiled, his eyes reflecting the depth of their conversation. "You're welcome, Michael. Remember, the journey of life is filled with unknowns, but it is in embracing those unknowns that we truly find ourselves. Venice awaits you with open arms. Embrace it, and you might find more than you ever imagined."

Michael nodded, a newfound determination in his heart. As he rose from the bench, he felt lighter, as if a burden had been lifted. The path before him might still be uncertain, but he was ready to face it with courage and an open heart.

Chapter 7

The upscale restaurant exuded elegance, with sophisticated, cinematic lighting that set the mood for a refined dining experience. The tables were adorned with pristine white tablecloths, gleaming silverware, and flickering candlelight, casting a warm and inviting glow. The ambiance was one of understated luxury, reminiscent of classic film noir.

Michael, accompanied by his friends, followed the waiter, Jack, to their table. Jack was a handsome, athletic man in his 30s, with a well-built and muscular frame beneath his suit and a charming mustache. His confident demeanor added to the allure of the evening. Liza was joined by Dave, a neurotic intellectual in his 30s, and Dave's partner Anna, a successful career woman in her 40s, who radiated confidence and sophistication.

"Isn't the lighting in here amazing?" Michael commented, taking in the elegant surroundings.

"It's like walking into a Bette Davis film," Anna agreed, her eyes sparkling with appreciation.

Liza, ever the sarcastic one, quipped, "I can't wait to see who gets slapped first."

Jack, the waiter, introduced himself with a flourish. "How do you do, I'm Jack. May I start you off with something to drink?"

"I'll have a gin martini, filthy, with three olives," Liza ordered, her voice playful yet decisive.

"Water's fine," Dave said, a hint of anxiety in his voice.

"Just a glass of *prosecco*," Anna requested, her tone calm and assured.

"I'll have the same," Michael added, feeling a bit more relaxed as Jack gave him a wink and walked away. Anna noticed the exchange and gave Michael a devious smile.

As they settled in, Michael decided to share his plans. "I think I'm going to go to Venice for a month."

Anna's eyebrows shot up. "What?"

"Yes. Do it! That sounds amazing!" Liza exclaimed, her enthusiasm palpable.

Dave, however, frowned in concern. "Venice? Really? Now? Aren't you worried about your emotional state?"

"Dave..." Anna interjected, rolling her eyes.

Michael sighed, feeling the weight of his decision. "I don't know. I just want to escape and forget about everything for a while."

Liza's eyes glazed over dreamily. "You know, I've always wanted to go to Italy. The men, the food, the wine... The men..."

Dave, always the pragmatist, nervously added, "Consider the flooding and the fact that the city is sinking."

"Oh, Dave, Venice isn't sinking tomorrow," Anna retorted, exasperated.

"But you know how romantic that place is," Dave insisted, turning to Michael. "You'll be surrounded by couples. It could make you feel awful."

Michael nodded thoughtfully. "Maybe, but that's the

point. I need to go. I need to see that life goes on."

Liza, smiling supportively, chimed in, "Well, if you're going to go soul-searching, Venice is as good a place as any."

"But what if you have a breakdown there? You won't have any friends or support system!" Dave fretted, his anxiety evident.

Anna placed a hand on Dave's arm. "Maybe you should consider taking someone with you. A travel companion who can be there for you."

Michael looked at Liza, an idea forming. "That's not a bad idea."

Liza's eyes widened with excitement. "Me? Oh my God..." She grabbed his hand. "I'd love to!"

Dave, panicking, tried to rein them in. "Hold on! Let's not get carried away here. What about your jobs, your responsibilities?"

"Oh, you're just jealous," Anna teased.

"I'm not jealous! I'm just... concerned," Dave defended, looking a bit flustered.

Michael appreciated Dave's concern but remained resolute. "I appreciate your concern, Dave. But I think a month in Venice could do wonders for me."

Liza grinned. "We'll send you pictures, Dave. And maybe bring you back some Murano glass."

"It'll probably break on the plane," Dave muttered, sulking.

Anna, trying to mediate, suggested, "You know what? Maybe Dave and I should join you guys. A group trip to Venice sounds like a blast."

Dave's eyes widened in panic. "What? No, no, no. I have work and, uh, my cat, and..."

Liza laughed, shaking her head. "Dave, you don't even

have a cat."

"Why go to Italy when I can just order the pasta right here, tonight?" Dave pointed to the menu. "Look, they've got penne."

"Dave, eating the penne here is not the same as wandering through ancient streets, tasting real gelato, and soaking up all the Italian... men," Liza retorted playfully.

Jack returned with their drinks, again catching Michael's eye. Michael felt a flutter of nerves but acknowledged the cruisy glance with a smile.

"You guys, if you want to come, I'd be thrilled. But there's no pressure," Michael said, addressing the table.

Anna considered the idea. "Let's give it some thought, Dave. Maybe we could join them for a week or so."

Dave, still anxious, mumbled, "Fine, but don't blame me when the city sinks!"

Liza raised her glass, a twinkle in her eye. "To *la dolce vita!*"

Everyone cheered *"la dolce vita,"* even Dave, who reluctantly joined in. The moment was filled with laughter and camaraderie, as the group envisioned their adventure in Venice.

As they continued their conversation, the waiter brought their appetizers, and the table was soon filled with delicious aromas. Liza took a sip of her martini, savoring the taste, and then looked at Michael with a thoughtful expression.

"Michael, what do you hope to find in Venice?" she asked, her voice softer and more serious than before.

Michael leaned back in his chair, contemplating her question. "I guess I'm looking for a fresh start. To remind myself that there's more to life than what I've been through. I want to rediscover who I am outside of all the chaos and heartbreak."

Anna nodded in understanding. "Sometimes, getting away from everything familiar is the best way to find yourself again."

Dave, still apprehensive but trying to be supportive, added, "Just make sure you stay safe and take care of yourself. And, you know, if you need anything, we're just a call away."

Liza reached across the table and squeezed Michael's hand. "You're going to have an amazing time, Michael. And who knows? Maybe you'll find more than just a fresh start."

Michael smiled, feeling a warmth spread through him at their support. "Thank you, guys. This means a lot to me."

As the evening progressed, the conversation flowed easily, filled with laughter, stories, and plans for the future. The friends shared their dreams and hopes, the bonds between them strengthening with each passing moment. By the time they finished their meal, Michael felt a renewed sense of hope and excitement for what lay ahead.

Jack returned to their table with the check, giving Michael one last wink before walking away. Michael watched him go, feeling a flutter of something new and exciting.

Anna, noticing his gaze, leaned in and whispered, "Looks like you might have a reason to come back here before you leave."

Michael chuckled, a blush creeping up his cheeks. "Maybe."

They all stood and made their way to the exit, the cool

night air greeting them as they stepped outside. The city lights twinkled around them, and the sounds of the evening created a comforting backdrop to their conversation.

As they said their goodbyes, Michael felt a sense of gratitude for his friends. He knew that no matter what happened in Venice, he had their unwavering support. And with that thought, he felt ready to embrace whatever the future held.

"To new beginnings," he said, raising an imaginary glass.

"To new beginnings," his friends echoed, their smiles lighting up the night.

Chapter 8

The evening had been filled with laughter, conversation, and the warmth of friendship. But now, in the quiet of the restaurant's coat room, the atmosphere was charged with a different kind of tension. Michael found himself in a moment of raw, unfiltered passion.

Jack, the waiter, was on his knees, his movements precise and deliberate. Michael gripped Jack's hair, his breaths coming in short, ragged gasps. The sensations built until he could no longer hold back, his body trembling as he orgasmed, groaning as quietly as he could.

"Oh fuck," Michael whispered, his voice a mix of relief and lingering desire.

Jack stood up, wiping his mouth with a casual, practiced motion. His eyes met Michael's, a mischievous glint in them. "I'm off at midnight if you wanna give me another load," he said, his voice low and inviting.

Michael felt a surge of adrenaline and excitement. The unexpected encounter left him breathless and exhilarated. He nodded, a small smile playing on his lips. "I'll be waiting," he replied, his voice steady despite the racing of his heart.

Jack grinned and straightened his uniform, the

moment of intimacy already fading into the background of his professional demeanor. "See you then," he said before slipping back into the bustling restaurant, leaving Michael alone in the coat room.

Michael took a deep breath, trying to steady himself. The intensity of the moment still lingered, a reminder of the impulsive choices that sometimes lead to the most unforgettable experiences. He adjusted his clothes and prepared to rejoin his friends, his mind a whirlwind of thoughts and emotions.

As he stepped out of the coat room, he was greeted by the familiar sights and sounds of the upscale restaurant. The elegant tables, the sophisticated lighting, and the hum of conversation all created a stark contrast to the heated encounter he had just experienced.

Making his way back to the table, Michael reflected on the night. The unexpected connection with Jack, the support of his friends, and the promise of a new beginning in Venice all swirled together, creating a tapestry of hope and anticipation.

He took his seat, feeling a renewed sense of purpose. The night may have taken an unexpected turn, but it also reminded him of the thrill of living in the moment, of embracing the unknown and finding passion in the most surprising places.

The rest of the evening unfolded with a sense of ease and contentment. Michael laughed with his friends, savoring the last moments of their time together. As the clock inched closer to midnight, he couldn't help but feel a sense of excitement for what the rest of the night—and the future—might hold.

When the time came to leave, Michael stepped out into the cool night air, his heart light and his spirit invigorated. He glanced back at the restaurant, knowing that this night was just the beginning of a journey filled with possibilities.

As he walked towards his car, he felt a sense of anticipation building within him. The promise of another encounter with Jack, the upcoming trip to Venice, and the unwavering support of his friends all combined to create a sense of hope and excitement.

Michael knew that life was unpredictable, filled with twists and turns that could lead to unexpected and unforgettable moments. And as he drove away, he felt ready to embrace whatever came next, confident in his ability to navigate the journey ahead.

Chapter 9

The room was dimly lit by a single lamp on the nightstand, casting soft shadows across the walls. Michael lay in bed naked, the warmth of recent intimacy still lingering in the air. Jack, equally naked, stood by the bed, hastily putting his clothes back on. The atmosphere was tense, filled with unspoken words and unresolved emotions.

"Wanna stay over? You don't have to go," Michael offered, his voice tinged with hope and vulnerability.

Jack, avoiding eye contact, continued to dress. "I gotta work tomorrow," he mumbled, the casual dismissal cutting through the quiet room.

Michael watched him, the hope in his eyes beginning to waver. "I'd love to see you again," he said, trying to keep his tone light but failing to mask the longing beneath.

Jack's movements became more hurried. "I don't know. I'm pretty busy with work," he replied, the words feeling like a practiced excuse.

Michael's heart sank further. He swallowed hard, forcing himself to ask, "When's your next day off?"

Jack finally looked at him, his expression firm and unyielding. "I'm not interested in pursuing anything more," he stated plainly, his tone devoid of emotion.

The impact of Jack's words hit Michael like a punch to the gut. His face fell, eyes brimming with disappointment and a deep sense of hurt. "Oh... I-I see," he stammered, his voice barely above a whisper as he tried to process the rejection.

Jack sighed, a hint of frustration in his voice. "Look, you seem like a nice guy. But I'm not into all that mushy, romantic crap. I'm just here for a good time, not a long time."

Michael felt a wave of sadness wash over him. The coldness and shallowness of Jack's words cut deeper than he expected. He watched as Jack finished dressing, feeling a growing sense of emptiness and isolation.

"Is that all it was to you?" Michael asked, his voice trembling with emotion. "Just a good time?"

Jack shrugged, not meeting his gaze. "Yeah. I mean, it was fun, but that's all it was. Don't take it personally."

Michael's eyes filled with tears, but he blinked them back, unwilling to let Jack see just how much this hurt. "I thought... I thought there was something more," he admitted, his voice breaking.

Jack paused for a moment, a flicker of something— perhaps regret or guilt—crossing his face. But it quickly vanished. "I'm sorry if you got the wrong idea," he said, his tone indifferent. "But I don't do relationships."

With that, Jack headed towards the door, each step echoing with finality. He paused for a moment, as if to say something more, but instead, he slammed the door behind him, the sound reverberating through the silence.

Left alone, Michael felt a crushing weight settle over him. The room felt colder, emptier. He lay back in the bed, staring up at the ceiling, his mind racing with a mix of emotions—hurt, anger, disappointment, and a profound sense of loneliness.

He turned over, clutching the pillow tightly as if it could offer some form of comfort. But the emptiness inside him only seemed to grow. Michael's thoughts drifted back to the brief moments of connection he thought he felt with Jack, the fleeting hope that maybe, just maybe, this could have been something more.

Tears finally spilled over, and he didn't bother to wipe them away. The pain of Jack's rejection cut deep, a stark reminder of the loneliness and longing that had plagued him since his breakup with Bernie. He thought he was ready to move on, to open himself up to new possibilities. But now, he felt more lost than ever.

He reached over to turn off the lamp, the room plunging into darkness. The silence was deafening, the emptiness overwhelming. Michael closed his eyes, willing himself to sleep, to escape the ache in his chest. But sleep didn't come easily. His mind was a whirlwind of thoughts and emotions, each one more painful than the last.

As the hours passed, Michael lay awake, grappling with his feelings. The night stretched on, long and lonely, filled with the echoes of Jack's cold words and the weight of his own heartache. And in the darkness, he felt the full weight of his solitude, the profound sense of being alone in a world that seemed increasingly indifferent to his pain.

Chapter 10

The plane landed smoothly on the runway, the rumble of the wheels a welcome end to the long journey. As the aircraft taxied to the gate, Michael looked out the window, taking in his first glimpses of Venice. His heart raced with a mix of excitement and apprehension. This trip felt like the beginning of something new, a chance to rediscover himself after the painful experiences of the past year.

Outside the airport, the group stood surrounded by their luggage. The warm sun cast a golden glow over everything, enhancing the vibrant colors of the city. The air was filled with the sounds of people speaking different languages, the hum of conversation blending with the distant calls of seagulls. The energy was palpable, a mix of excitement and anticipation as they prepared to embark on their Venetian adventure.

"I can't believe we're actually here!" Liza exclaimed, her eyes sparkling with joy.

"We just need to find our speedboat taxi thing to the hotel," Anna said, consulting a map.

"Speedboat? You mean we're not taking a regular taxi?" Dave frowned, his concern evident.

"Dave, this is Venice. It's all about the boats here. No

cars, no regular taxis. Just water taxis and *gondolas*," Liza laughed, shaking her head.

Michael stood a bit apart from the group, his thoughts racing. The sight of the canals and the historic buildings rising out of the water filled him with a sense of awe. The beauty of Venice was almost surreal, like stepping into a dream. He took a deep breath, trying to absorb the reality of being here, of starting this new chapter in his life.

As they made their way to the dock, the sounds and sights of Venice became more pronounced. The gentle lapping of water against the stone walls, the soft murmur of Italian spoken all around, and the intricate architecture that told stories of centuries past. Michael felt a sense of wonder, mixed with a tinge of nervousness about what lay ahead.

They reached the dock where a sleek speedboat taxi awaited. The driver, a friendly-looking man with a weathered face, helped them load their luggage. "*Buongiorno!* Welcome to Venice!" he greeted them with a warm smile.

"*Buongiorno!*" they echoed, their excitement building.

As the speedboat rocketed across the lagoon between *Venezia* and the airport, the wind caressed Michael's face, whispering secrets of the ancient city that lay ahead. The boat's engine created a lulling melody, blending with the rhythmic sound of the water.

The ancient city emerged from the veil of sea mist, an ethereal apparition hovering between water and sky. Venice, a city suspended in time, its beauty both arresting and fragile. *Gondolas* and *vaporettos* meandered through the waterways, the rhythm of their journey echoing the heartbeat of the city.

As they entered the winding canals, the speed of the

boat subsided, allowing Michael to absorb the details of his surroundings. The intricate lacework of bridges arching over the water, the delicate dance of light on the surface of the canals, and the patina of history etched into the facades of the *palazzos* all wove together into a tapestry of enchantment.

The whisper of the wind gave way to the melodic lilt of laughter and conversation that spilled from the narrow streets, imbuing the city with a vibrant energy. The scent of the sea mingled with that of fresh bread, aged stone, and the faintest hint of flowers blooming on hidden terraces.

As the boat approached the dock of their hotel, a final sense of anticipation filled Michael's chest, like the crescendo of a symphony reaching its peak. The hotel itself, nestled against the water, offered a sanctuary in the midst of the city's mysterious embrace.

Michael stepped onto the dock, his heart swelling with the promise of adventure and discovery that awaited him within the narrow alleys and sun-dappled squares.

As the sun set, bathing the city in a warm embrace, the enchanting song of Venice began to play, and Michael was swept away by the melody.

The hotel lobby was a realm of timeless allure and enchantment. The space radiated an aura of elegance, capturing the essence of a bygone era where luxury and refinement were paramount. The lobby was a sanctuary, an oasis of tranquility amidst the vibrant energy of Venice. The warm glow of delicate chandeliers bathed the room in a soft, golden light, casting a mesmerizing dance of shadows upon the exquisite floors. Ornate columns rose towards the high ceilings, adorned with intricate details that spoke of a rich and storied past.

The air was redolent with the scent of fresh flowers, their fragrance delicately intermingling with the soft notes of classical music that wafted through the air. Plush furnishings invited weary travelers to sink into their embrace, providing a respite from the bustling streets outside.

It was a hideaway where time seemed to stand still, a place where memories were woven into the very fabric of the walls. Stepping into this palace of historic elegance, Michael and his companions found themselves embraced by the exquisite ambiance, knowing that they had arrived at a sanctuary where their Venetian journey would unfold in unforgettable ways.

Exhausted from the transatlantic travel, they headed off to their rooms, eager to rest and recharge for the adventures that lay ahead. Michael took one last look around the lobby, feeling a sense of peace settle over him. This was the beginning of something new, a chance to find himself in the heart of Venice.

Chapter 11

Michael's hotel room was a sanctuary of serenity, a haven where he could retreat from the bustling city and find solace in the embrace of luxury. As he entered, he was greeted by an ambiance of refined elegance, where every detail had been thoughtfully curated to create an atmosphere of timeless beauty.

The room exuded a sense of understated grandeur, with its tastefully appointed furnishings and rich fabrics that draped gracefully across the space. The gentle play of natural light filtered through the windows, casting a soft glow that illuminated the room with a delicate radiance. The hues of the Venetian sunset began to paint the room in shades of gold and amber, adding to its ethereal charm.

An inviting bed stood as the centerpiece of the room, adorned with sumptuous linens and pillows that promised nights of sweet dreams. The mattress felt plush yet supportive, beckoning Michael to sink into its comfort. The polished furniture exuded a sense of timeless craftsmanship, each piece meticulously chosen to complement the room's sophisticated decor. Elegant artwork adorned the walls, depicting scenes of Venetian canals and *gondolas*, further immersing him in the local culture.

Michael began to unpack, each item finding its place in the room. As he placed his clothes in the wardrobe and arranged his toiletries in the bathroom, the hushed atmosphere enveloped him, offering a respite from the outside world and providing a sense of serenity that allowed him to fully immerse himself in the Venetian experience.

Curious and somewhat lonely, he checked in on Grindr, scrolling through the profiles of men in the area. The app buzzed with activity, showcasing a diverse array of potential connections. He exchanged a few casual messages, feeling the excitement of possibility mingling with his lingering apprehensions. Yet, he didn't feel the urgency to meet anyone tonight. He just enjoyed the thought of being noticed, of being desired in this new city.

After a few minutes, he set his phone aside and stripped off his travel-worn clothes. The cool air of the room was refreshing against his skin. He stepped into the bathroom, the spacious shower offering a cascade of warm water that soothed his tired muscles. The water flowed over him, washing away the fatigue of travel and the remnants of his past worries. He took his time, relishing the moment of solitude and self-care.

Clean and refreshed, Michael dried off and climbed into the inviting bed. The linens felt like a soft embrace, the pillows cradling his head as he settled in. He pulled the blanket over himself, feeling the day's weariness begin to melt away. The sounds of the city outside were distant and muted, adding to the peaceful cocoon of his room.

As he lay there, he thought about the journey that

brought him here, the friends who supported him, and the unknown adventures that awaited. He felt a blend of anticipation and calm, ready to face whatever came next. With a contented sigh, he closed his eyes, allowing himself to drift into a deep, restorative sleep, the promise of Venice waiting for him in his dreams.

Chapter 12

Michael woke the next morning to the harmonious clamor of church bells. It felt as if the whole city was alive with sound, each bell contributing its unique voice to the morning symphony. The bells echoed from every direction, their tones resonating through the walls of his hotel room and into his very bones.

Still groggy from sleep, Michael stretched and got out of bed. The sumptuous linens fell away, revealing the warmth and comfort they had provided throughout the night. He made his way to the enormous windows that dominated one side of the room. With a sense of anticipation, he pulled back the heavy curtains, letting the early morning light flood in.

He unlocked the windows and pushed them open, leaning out into the fresh Venetian air. The cool breeze carried with it the scent of the sea mixed with the aroma of freshly baked bread and brewing coffee from the nearby cafes. Below, the canals reflected the morning light, shimmering like liquid silver.

The bells continued their relentless chorus, a cacophony of exquisite chimes and tones that blended together in a mesmerizing melody. Michael stood there for a moment, letting the sounds wash over him, feeling a sense of peace and wonder. It was as if the city itself was welcoming him, its ancient voice speaking directly to his heart.

Reaching for his phone, Michael decided to capture this moment. He began recording, hoping to preserve the magic of this Venetian morning. The screen showed the waves of sound, each bell's tone distinct yet part of a greater whole. He imagined sharing this recording with his friends back home, allowing them to experience a piece of the beauty he was witnessing.

As he recorded, Michael's mind drifted. The church bells reminded him of the passage of time, each chime marking a second, a minute, a moment that would never come again. He thought about the journey that brought him here, the heartbreak and the healing, and the promise of new beginnings.

The sun continued to rise, casting long shadows and bathing the city in a warm glow. Michael turned his gaze to the streets below, watching as the city came to life. *Gondolas* glided gracefully along the canals, their passengers wrapped in the same sense of awe that he felt. Vendors set up their stalls, preparing for the day's business, while locals and tourists alike began to fill the cobblestone pathways.

Michael took a deep breath, savoring the unique blend of sounds, sights, and smells. This was what he came for—a chance to lose himself in the beauty and history of Venice, to find solace in its rhythms and rediscover parts of himself that he thought were lost forever.

He ended the recording and placed his phone on the windowsill, reluctant to pull himself away from the view. But the day awaited, and he felt a sense of excitement building within him. Today, he would explore the winding alleys and hidden squares, the grand *palazzos* and humble *trattorias*. He would let the city guide him, each step an invitation to discover something new.

Michael dressed quickly, choosing comfortable clothes that would allow him to wander without restriction. He grabbed a light jacket, knowing the weather could change unexpectedly. With one last glance out the window, he stepped back into his room, ready to embark on his Venetian adventure.

As he headed out the door, Michael felt a renewed sense of purpose. The bells had given him a gift—an awakening to the possibilities that lay ahead. And with that, he set off into the heart of Venice, eager to embrace whatever the day had in store.

Chapter 13

Outside the hotel, Michael lit a cigarette and sipped an espresso. The morning air was crisp and invigorating, filled with the rich aromas of coffee and the distant scent of the sea. He leaned against the wrought iron railing, taking in the scene of the waking city. The streets were beginning to fill with locals and tourists alike, each person contributing to the vibrant tapestry of Venetian life.

"Buongiorno!" Liza's cheerful voice broke his reverie. She approached, her own cigarette in hand, a playful smile on her lips.

"Morning gorgeous," Michael replied, his face lighting up. They exchanged a quick kiss on each cheek, the European way.

"How'd you sleep?" he asked, genuinely curious.

"Like a boulder," Liza laughed, taking a long drag of her cigarette. She joined him at the railing, their elbows almost touching.

"These beds are divine. How about you?" she continued, blowing out a puff of smoke.

"Same. I'm in love with the pillows. I haven't slept that well in a long time," Michael admitted, savoring another sip of his espresso.

They stood in comfortable silence for a moment, watching the city come to life around them. *Gondolas* glided silently through the canals, the *gondoliers'* soft songs adding a musical backdrop to the morning.

"You know," Liza said thoughtfully, "there's something about Venice that feels like a dream. It's so different from anywhere else."

Michael nodded, flicking ash from his cigarette. "Yeah, it's like stepping into another world. Everything here feels... timeless."

"I think that's why it's such a great place to escape to," Liza mused. "You can leave all your worries behind and just... be."

Michael smiled at her words, feeling a sense of agreement deep within. "I think that's exactly what I needed. A break from reality."

They finished their cigarettes and Michael gestured to a nearby café. "Shall we get another round of these?" he suggested, holding up his empty espresso cup.

"Absolutely," Liza agreed, linking her arm through his. They strolled to the café, their footsteps echoing lightly on the cobblestones.

As they sat down at a small table outside the café, a waiter promptly appeared to take their order. "Two espressos, *per favore*," Michael said, his Italian accent improving with practice.

Liza looked around, her eyes sparkling with excitement. "What do you want to do today? There's so much to see and explore."

Michael considered for a moment. "I was thinking of just wandering around, getting lost in the streets. Maybe visit some of the lesser-known spots."

Liza nodded enthusiastically. "That sounds perfect.

And we definitely need to try some authentic Venetian cuisine. I've heard there's a place nearby that does amazing *bigoi co' l'arna*."

Their conversation flowed easily, filled with plans and shared excitement for the day ahead. The waiter returned with their espressos, and they clinked their tiny cups together in a toast.

"To adventure," Liza said with a grin.

"To adventure," Michael echoed, feeling the warmth of the coffee spread through him.

They lingered over their drinks, soaking in the ambiance of the bustling café. The morning sun climbed higher in the sky, casting a golden glow over everything. The bells from the nearby churches continued their occasional chime, a gentle reminder of the city's rhythm.

Michael felt a sense of contentment settle over him. He was grateful for this moment, for the chance to explore and rediscover himself in such a magical place. As they finished their espressos and prepared to start their day, he knew that this was just the beginning of an unforgettable adventure in Venice.

Chapter 14

As the sun climbed higher in the sky, casting its golden embrace upon the city, Michael, Liza, Dave, and Anna ventured forth into the labyrinth of Venice. Together, they stepped through the narrow passages and emerged into the beating heart of the city, the fabled *Piazza San Marco*. St. Mark's Square, with its timeless grandeur, seemed to pause and hold its breath as the friends entered. They marveled at the towering *Campanile*, a proud sentinel watching over the city from its lofty perch, while the grand façade of St. Mark's *Basilica* unfolded before them like a treasure chest, brimming with stories of the past, its mosaic-adorned domes shimmering with silent devotion.

The four friends, bewitched by the enchantment of the square, wove through the tourists and locals, pausing to admire the elegance of the *Doge's* Palace, a masterpiece of medieval architecture that looked like a cake. They watched, captivated, as the pigeons swooped and swirled, their wings rustling like the pages of a living storybook.

Orchestras from the historic cafés filled the air, their notes spilling across the square like delicate petals on a breeze. Laughter mingled with the scent of espresso and the distant echo of footsteps on the cobblestones.

Michael stopped in his tracks, overwhelmed by the sheer magnitude of the *Piazza*. "This place is like a living museum," he said, his voice filled with awe.

Liza nodded, her eyes sparkling. "It's like stepping into a different time. You can almost feel the history."

They walked slowly, taking in every detail. The intricate carvings on the façade of St. Mark's *Basilica* seemed to tell stories of saints and angels, while the golden mosaics caught the sunlight, making the entire structure gleam with an almost divine light. The *Campanile* stood tall and proud, offering a panoramic view of the city for those who dared to climb its heights.

"Look at the *Doge's* Palace," Anna said, pointing to the elegant building. "It looks like a piece of art itself."

Dave took out his camera, eager to capture the beauty around him. "This place is a photographer's dream," he said, snapping photos of the *basilica*, the *Campanile*, and the lively scenes around them.

They made their way to the center of the square, where the orchestras from the historic cafés played timeless melodies. The music filled the air, adding a magical quality to the already enchanting atmosphere. They found a spot to sit and watch the world go by, soaking in the ambiance of one of the most beautiful squares in the world.

The aroma of fresh pastries from a nearby bakery tempted them, and Michael bought a bag of warm, sugary *fritole*, sharing them with the group. The sweet treats melted in their mouths, adding to the sensory delight of the morning.

"These are delicious," Liza said, savoring each bite. "I could eat these all day."

As they munched on the *fritole*, they watched the pigeons dance around the square. Children chased after them, their laughter ringing out like a joyful chorus. Artists set up their easels, capturing the beauty of the square on their canvases. Street performers entertained small crowds, their talents adding to the lively atmosphere.

The friends took a leisurely stroll around the square, exploring its many corners. They admired the ornate lampposts that lined the walkways, each one a work of art in itself. The grand statues that adorned the square stood as silent sentinels, watching over the city with a regal air.

They found themselves drawn to the café orchestras, their music a siren call that beckoned them closer. The friends took a seat at one of the outdoor tables, ordering cappuccinos and enjoying the live performance. The musicians played with passion and skill, their melodies weaving through the air like a delicate tapestry.

Michael closed his eyes, letting the music wash over him. "This is exactly what I needed," he said, a contented smile on his face.

Anna sipped her cappuccino, her eyes closed in bliss. "This moment is perfect," she agreed. "I feel like we've stepped into a different world."

The sun continued its ascent, casting a warm, golden light over the square. The reflections of the buildings danced on the surface of the canal, creating a mesmerizing display of light and color. The square became even more vibrant as the day progressed, with more vendors setting up stalls selling everything from handcrafted jewelry to Venetian masks.

Michael stopped at one of the stalls, fascinated by the

intricate designs of the masks. He picked up a deep blue one adorned with silver filigree and feathers, turning it over in his hands.

"Thinking of getting one?" Liza asked, joining him.

Michael smiled. "Maybe. It would be a nice reminder of this trip."

They continued to explore the square, taking in every detail. Each corner offered something new and fascinating, from the grand statues to the ornate lampposts that lined the walkways. The history of the square felt palpable, as if the very stones beneath their feet were whispering tales of the past.

As the sun began to set, casting a warm, golden light over the square, the friends found a spot by the water's edge to rest. The reflections of the buildings danced on the surface of the canal, creating a mesmerizing display of light and color. The orchestras played on, their music mingling with the soft murmur of the crowd and the gentle lapping of the water against the stones.

"Today has been perfect," Michael said, his voice filled with contentment.

"And it's just the beginning," Liza added, smiling. "There's so much more to see and do."

Michael looked around at his friends, feeling a deep sense of gratitude. This trip was exactly what he needed—a chance to reconnect with himself and with the world. As they sat together, sharing stories and laughter, he knew that these moments would become cherished memories, etched forever in the heart of Venice.

Chapter 15

As twilight descended upon the enchanting city, Michael found himself wandering alone through the labyrinth of narrow streets and shadowed alleys, the gentle pulse of Venice guiding his steps. The city's beauty took on a darker, more mysterious tone as the fading light cast long, eerie shadows. The cobblestones under his feet were slick with a thin sheen of moisture, reflecting the dim glow of the street lamps.

The air was thick with the scent of the canals, a mix of brine and damp stone, mingling with the faint aroma of distant dinners being prepared. The sounds of the city were muffled, the lively chatter of tourists replaced by the quiet whispers of the night. Michael felt a thrill of excitement and a touch of apprehension as he delved deeper into the maze of Venice's streets.

As he meandered, Michael's eyes fell upon a handsome young man leaning against a weathered wall, his gaze holding a secret, a whispered invitation to something thrilling. The man, with dark hair and piercing eyes, exuded an air of danger and allure.

Their eyes met, and the electric charge between them crackled with a silent dance of desire and intrigue. Michael's heart quickened, and he felt an irresistible pull towards the stranger. With a subtle tilt of his head, the young man beckoned Michael to follow him. The pull of desire and the mystery of the unknown guided Michael deeper into the city's shadowy embrace.

The stranger led him down a secluded alleyway, removed from the hum of tourists. The walls closed in, narrowing the path until it felt as though they were the only two people in the world. The air grew cooler, the shadows deeper. Michael could hear his own heartbeat, a steady drum in the silence of the night.

As they stood in the shadows, the handsome stranger drew nearer, the electricity between them intensifying. Their breaths mingled in the cool air, the anticipation almost unbearable. Finally, their lips met in a fever pitch, a desperate clash of desire and need.

Hands roamed and breaths quickened as the world beyond the confines of the alley slipped away into insignificance. It was fleeting and quick, yet charged with an intensity that left Michael breathless. He felt the stranger's hands on his body, guiding him with a confidence that spoke of experience.

Michael unbuttoned Angelo's pants and dropped to his knees, his hands trembling with a mix of excitement and nerves. He engulfed Angelo, who moaned quietly, his sounds echoing off the narrow walls. The saltiness, the feel of the hard thickness, the raw intimacy of the moment consumed Michael, each sensation heightened by the risk and the secrecy.

Michael kept sucking and licking.

Angelo let out a deep guttural moan, his hips bucking forward, hands gripping the sides of Michael's head.

Suddenly, a noise nearby—a clatter of footsteps, the distant murmur of voices—caused Angelo to panic. His eyes widened in fear, and he stuffed his dick back into his pants, zipped up, and ran off into the shadows without a word. Michael, left in the cold grip of abandonment, panted heavily as he wiped his mouth, his heart still racing from the encounter.

He stood, looking around to find out if anyone had seen him. The alleyway was empty, the shadows long and silent. The thrill of the moment gave way to a sense of vulnerability and exposure. He felt the weight of the night pressing in on him, the darkness more oppressive now that he was alone.

Michael leaned against the wall, his mind a whirlwind of emotions. He felt a mix of exhilaration and shame, desire and regret. The thrill of the encounter was tainted by the sudden, abrupt end, leaving him feeling hollow. He pushed himself off the wall and slowly made his way back towards the lights and the safety of the busier streets, the echo of Angelo's departure haunting him.

As he stepped back into the light, the normalcy of the city seemed jarring. The sounds of laughter and conversation, the clinking of glasses, the distant strains of music—all served as a stark contrast to the dark, intimate moment he had just experienced. Michael felt a shiver run through him, a lingering sense of unease as he navigated his way back to the hotel.

The encounter, though brief, had left a mark on him. He couldn't shake the image of Angelo's eyes, the intensity of their connection, the abruptness of the ending. As he reached the hotel, he paused for a moment, looking back at the direction he came from, the shadows of the alleys now holding a different kind of mystery.

With a deep breath, he stepped inside, the warmth and light of the hotel wrapping around him like a protective cloak. The city outside continued its rhythm, but Michael knew that something within him had shifted, the night's events leaving him with more questions than answers.

Chapter 16

Michael entered the hotel lobby, looking both exhilarated and slightly disheveled. The warm lighting and elegant decor offered a stark contrast to the dark, suspenseful streets he had just wandered through. Liza, sitting at the bar and flirting with the handsome Italian bartender, noticed Michael and called him over with a playful grin.

"You look like you've been up to something," Liza teased, her eyes sparkling with curiosity.

Michael hesitated for a moment before joining Liza at the bar. He avoided eye contact, a hint of shame and sadness on his face. "Oh, I was just, uh, exploring. You know, soaking in the ambiance," he lied, trying to mask his recent experience.

Liza, perceptive as always, saw through his facade. She offered him a knowing smile. "That's great... Want a glass of wine?"

"Yeah," Michael replied, his voice subdued.

Liza looked at Michael, recognizing the sadness in his eyes. She reached out and placed her hand on his knee, offering her support. She noticed it was a bit damp and dirty from kneeling on the cobblestones moments earlier. "I'm so happy we're here," she said softly.

Michael forced a weak smile. "Totally. I'm delirious. Wine sounds good and then to bed. Jetlag sucks."

Liza nodded, gave him a reassuring squeeze on the hand before turning her attention back to the bartender, her flirtatious grin returning. "Do you have Soave?" she asked.

"*Si*," the bartender replied with a charming smile.

"Great. A Soave for my friend and I'll have another of the same," Liza ordered, her eyes twinkling.

The bartender poured Michael's glass of wine and handed it to him. "*Grazie*," Michael muttered, taking a sip and savoring the crisp, refreshing taste.

Liza continued her playful banter with the bartender. "What's the secret to making the perfect Bellini?" she asked, her tone flirtatious.

The bartender, his smile widening, leaned in closer. "*Eh, bella signorina, capisci*, the secret lies in the perfect balance between the juiciest, most succulent peaches and the finest, most premium *Prosecco*. But let me tell you, the true magic lies in the skilled hands of the bartender. Shall I show you how it's done?"

"I'd be delighted. Show me your skills, *signore*," Liza replied, her voice low and enticing.

The bartender proceeded to expertly make a Bellini, his eyes locked on Liza's, as if performing a seductive dance. His movements were fluid and precise, each gesture exuding confidence and charm.

As Liza and the sexy bartender continued flirting, Michael decided to join in, attempting to flirt with the bartender as well. "You must have learned from the best," he said, trying to catch the bartender's attention.

The bartender, however, remained focused on Liza, clearly more interested in her. He barely acknowledged

Michael's comment, his attention fully captivated by Liza. *"Ah, bella signorina,* I learned from the best. My teacher was a legendary bartender in her time. She passed her secrets down to me," he said, his eyes never leaving Liza's.

Liza giggled, her cheeks flushing with excitement. "I must say, watching you work is mesmerizing."

The bartender grinned, a mischievous glint in his eyes. *"Ah, bella signorina,* you flatter me."

As Michael watched Liza and the bartender, he couldn't help but feel a twinge of jealousy, wishing he had someone to share a flirtatious moment with as well. But the bartender's lack of interest in Michael, as well as his recent escapade and the complicated emotions that came with it, weighed heavily on his mind, making it difficult for him to fully engage in the light-hearted atmosphere around him.

He took another sip of his wine, trying to drown out the conflicting feelings swirling within him. The warmth of the wine soothed him slightly, but the nagging sense of loneliness remained. He glanced around the lobby, observing the other hotel guests chatting and laughing, their lives seemingly uncomplicated compared to his.

Liza, noticing Michael's distant expression, placed a gentle hand on his arm. "Hey, are you okay?" she asked softly, her concern evident.

Michael forced a smile. "Yeah, I'm fine. Just a bit tired," he lied again.

Liza didn't push him further. She understood that he needed time to process whatever he was going through. "Alright, but if you need to talk, I'm here," she said, squeezing his arm reassuringly.

"Thanks, Liza," Michael replied, genuinely

appreciating her support.

The bartender finished making the Bellini and handed it to Liza with a flourish. "For the *bella signorina*," he said with a wink.

Liza took the drink, her eyes sparkling with delight. "*Grazie*," she said, raising her glass to the bartender.

Michael raised his glass as well, attempting to join in the celebratory mood. "Cheers," he said, his voice lacking its usual enthusiasm.

As they sipped their drinks, the lively atmosphere of the bar contrasted sharply with Michael's inner turmoil. He tried to focus on the pleasant buzz of the alcohol and the lively chatter around him, but his thoughts kept drifting back to the shadowy encounter in the alley and the complex emotions it stirred within him.

Eventually, the fatigue from the day's adventures and the emotional strain caught up with him. He set his empty glass on the bar and looked at Liza. "I think I'm going to head to bed. I'll see you in the morning."

Liza nodded, her eyes filled with understanding. "Goodnight, Michael. Sleep well."

Michael gave her a small smile before turning and making his way to the elevator. As he ascended to his room, he felt the weight of the night's events pressing down on him. He knew he needed to confront his feelings and find a way to navigate the complexities of his emotions, but for now, all he wanted was the solace of sleep.

He entered his room, the familiar surroundings providing a sense of comfort. He undressed and climbed into bed, the soft linens and plush pillows offering a welcome embrace. As he closed his eyes, the memories of the day played through his mind, a mix of beauty, excitement, and lingering sadness. He took a deep breath, allowing himself to relax, and slowly drifted off to sleep, hoping that tomorrow would bring clarity and peace.

Chapter 17

The clamor of church bells echoing throughout the city stirred Michael from his sleep, their resonant peals announcing the dawn of a new day. The sun, its warm rays stealing through the cracks in the curtains, cast a golden glow upon the room. The warm, comforting light gradually pulled Michael from his slumber, the softness of the bed and the luxurious sheets a pleasant contrast to the awakening bustle of Venice outside.

Rubbing the sleep from his eyes, Michael reached for his phone, curiosity tugging at him as he opened Grindr. He scrolled through his messages, noting the faceless profiles and indecipherable Italian greetings with a faint sense of detachment. Each message felt like a whisper in a foreign language, distant and impersonal, failing to penetrate the lingering shadows of his mind from the night before.

But then, as if conjured by fate, Michael stumbled upon the profile of a handsome man named Marco. His captivating eyes and playful smile seemed to leap from the screen, igniting a spark of interest within Michael's chest. Marco's profile, eloquently crafted in perfect English, painted a picture of a charming and adventurous soul. The bio read, "Wanderer, dreamer, lover of life. Let's explore the hidden corners of Venice together."

Hesitating only for a moment, Michael composed a message, his fingers tapping against the screen with an eager rhythm. His message was simple yet sincere: "Hi Marco, your profile caught my eye. I'd love to explore Venice with you. How about coffee today?" As he hit send, a sense of anticipation filled him, a flutter of excitement stirring in his stomach.

The minutes passed like hours as he awaited a reply, each chime of the church bells only serving to heighten his anticipation. He paced the room, occasionally glancing out the window at the bustling city below, wondering about the man on the other side of the screen. The anticipation built, the silence of the room amplifying his every thought and hope.

And then, his phone sprang to life with a ding. Michael's heart skipped a beat as he picked it up, reading Marco's reply: "Hi Michael! I'd love to meet you. There's a cozy café off the beaten path, perfect for a quiet chat. How about 10 AM?"

Michael smiled, a sense of relief and excitement washing over him. He quickly replied, "Sounds perfect. See you there!" The exchange felt like the beginning of something promising, a new adventure in this beautiful city.

Michael headed to the bathroom, freshening up with a quick shower. The warm water cascaded over him, washing away the remnants of sleep and the lingering unease from the previous night's encounter. As he dressed, he chose his outfit carefully, wanting to make a good impression. He opted for a casual yet stylish look, perfect for a morning coffee date.

Chapter 18

The hotel's breakfast room was a vision of elegance, bathed in soft morning light that streamed through beautiful windows. It was a space where indulgence met sophistication, a sanctuary of culinary delights that set the stage for a memorable start to the day. The aroma of freshly baked pastries mingled with the rich scent of espresso, creating an inviting atmosphere that beckoned the guests to relax and enjoy.

Michael sat at a polished wooden table, a steaming cup of espresso in hand. He sipped slowly, savoring the bold flavor. The room hummed with the gentle murmur of conversations, punctuated by the occasional clink of cutlery against porcelain. His friends, Liza, Dave, and Anna, joined him, their plates filled with an array of breakfast options from the lavish buffet.

"You know," Michael began, breaking the comfortable silence, "I really love these dating apps. They let you screen people before actually meeting them in person. I typically message a guy who seems interesting, and if he's up for it, we'll meet in public for coffee."

Liza, sitting next to him, nodded in agreement while nibbling on a croissant. "That makes sense. It's a good way to feel things out first."

Michael continued, "If they won't meet in public, I just end the conversation. They're probably married, not out, or catfishing."

Dave, ever the pessimist, chimed in with a smirk. "Or a serial killer on the hunt, or maybe even a bigoted homophobic gang."

Anna rolled her eyes at Dave's dramatic tone. "Oh, Dave."

He shrugged, unfazed. "You never know these days."

Michael chuckled. "Well, I prefer to focus on the positive aspects. Besides, the app completely eliminates the need to go to a bar to meet someone."

Dave leaned back in his chair, folding his arms. "Right, it's a bit like ordering food from a delivery menu."

Liza, always supportive, offered a balanced perspective. "Well, it's nice to go to a bar and meet people in person. But you're right, it does save a lot of valuable time. Apps let you bypass all the nonsense that usually comes with dating. I'm on vacation. I don't have time. It's quite efficient, really."

Michael nodded appreciatively. "Anyway, so I came across this profile for a guy named Marco, and after a little back-and-forth, he invited me to coffee."

Liza perked up, her eyes sparkling with curiosity. "When? We should be there for backup in case he turns out to be a nightmare."

Dave, unable to resist, added, "Or a murderer."

Michael laughed, shaking his head. "I can handle myself."

Anna placed a reassuring hand on Michael's arm. "We know you can, Michael. We just want to make sure you're safe. That's all."

"Fine," Michael conceded with a smile. "You can come, but you have to promise to be discreet."

Liza grinned, raising her coffee cup in a mock salute. "Of course! We won't even look at you!"

Dave, not missing a beat, echoed her sentiment with playful sarcasm. "Oh, absolutely. We'll be practically invisible."

The friends shared a laugh, the camaraderie and mutual care evident in their interactions. The breakfast room buzzed with life, the sunlight streaming in and casting a warm glow over their table. As they finished their breakfast, the excitement for the day ahead built.

Michael felt a mixture of nerves and anticipation about meeting Marco. The support and humor of his friends eased his anxiety, reminding him that he wasn't alone in this new adventure. Together, they made plans for the day, deciding to explore more of Venice before Michael's coffee date.

As they left the breakfast room, the city's charm awaited them outside, promising a day filled with discoveries and new experiences. For Michael, the prospect of meeting Marco added an extra layer of excitement, a hint of the unknown that made his heart race with eager anticipation.

Chapter 19

Michael settled nervously into his seat at the quaint café, the warm sun casting a soft glow on the narrow street. His friends sat at a nearby table, their eyes flickering with curiosity as they attempted to feign nonchalance. The café was a charming hideaway, its tables adorned with fresh flowers and the soft murmur of conversation creating a cozy atmosphere.

Michael's gaze darted repeatedly towards the winding path, each approaching figure igniting a spark of hope that it might be Marco. The anticipation was palpable, the seconds stretching into what felt like minutes. The aroma of freshly brewed coffee mingled with the scent of baked pastries, adding to the sensory delight of the moment.

Amidst the buzz of conversation and the aroma of freshly brewed coffee, Michael's anticipation built. The minutes ticked by on his watch, punctuated by the gentle laughter of patrons and the occasional clink of a cup. He took a deep breath, trying to calm his nerves, reminding himself that this was just a coffee date, not an interrogation.

Then, as if by some divine signal, Michael caught sight of a figure rushing towards him, and his heart leaped with recognition. Marco had arrived, adorned in the finest attire. A cashmere scarf draped around his neck, a wool overcoat hinting at his athletic build. His demeanor was one of elegance and intelligence, reminiscent of a university professor. The way he carried himself, with an air of confidence and grace, immediately put Michael at ease.

As Marco neared, Michael's nerves began to dissipate, replaced by a spark of connection between them. Marco's eyes locked onto Michael's, and his expression became one of warmth. The moment felt electric, as if the universe had aligned just for them.

"Michael, it's wonderful to meet you," Marco said, his voice smooth and inviting.

"Likewise, Marco," Michael replied, his smile genuine and welcoming. "Thank you for meeting me."

As Marco joined Michael at the table, they exchanged greetings, their voices harmonizing with the melodic backdrop of the café. The initial awkwardness faded quickly as they began to talk, their conversation flowing naturally. Michael found himself captivated by Marco's charm and intellect.

From their point of view, Michael's friends watched with approval and delight, witnessing the chemistry blossoming between the two men. Liza, Anna, and Dave sat close enough to observe, yet far enough to give Michael some privacy.

"He's so handsome!" Liza whispered, her eyes twinkling with excitement.

Anna nodded in agreement. "Absolutely. He has such a distinguished look."

Dave, however, looked nervous. "What if he's in the mafia or something?" he muttered, his imagination running wild.

Liza rolled her eyes, whispering back, "Dave, not every Italian is in the mafia."

Dave remained skeptical. "I don't know. You hear stories."

Anna teased him, "Dave, you watch too many movies. Relax, will you?"

They continued to watch Michael and Marco, their curiosity mingled with genuine happiness for their friend. The chemistry between Michael and Marco was undeniable, and it became increasingly clear that this encounter was more than just a casual meeting.

Chapter 20

Michael and Marco sat at their table, sipping espressos. Michael was visibly nervous, his fingers tapping lightly against the porcelain cup. Marco's charm and warm demeanor helped calm his nerves, making the conversation flow naturally.

"Tell me," Marco said with a smile, "what is your favorite thing about *Venezia* so far?"

Michael took a moment to think. "I think it's the way the city seems to seduce you at every turn. The winding canals, the mysterious alleyways... It's all so seductive and... tempting."

"Ah, indeed, a city of temptations," Marco agreed, grinning. "It has a way of drawing you in and making you crave more. Have you tried our famous gelato?"

"Not yet," Michael admitted, his curiosity piqued.

"It's rich, creamy, and simply melts in your mouth," Marco said, his voice dropping to a flirtatious tone.

Michael blushed slightly. "I can't wait. Maybe you can show me your favorite place?"

"It would be my pleasure," Marco replied, leaning in closer. "Just be prepared – once you've had a taste, you'll never want to stop."

"Venice seems like the perfect place to explore all

kinds of things," Michael said, leaning in as well.

Marco's eyes locked onto Michael's, and his voice lowered to a mesmerizing whisper. "*Venezia*, my dear friend, is a living, breathing work of art. Passion flows through its canals like blood through our veins. In every corner, you will find mystery and seduction. The shadows hold secrets that only the bravest souls dare to uncover."

Marco's words wove a spell around Michael, drawing him in deeper. "Here, the spirit of Casanova, the legendary lover, lingers on. He was a man who understood the importance of pleasure. He was driven by an insatiable hunger for new experiences and an undying thirst for the carnal delights of the flesh. Just like the great Casanova, we too can surrender ourselves to the sensuous temptations of *Venezia*."

"We can lose ourselves in the labyrinth of desires," Marco continued, his voice now a soft, hypnotic murmur. "Where every touch, every taste, every whisper is a tantalizing invitation to explore the depths of our own spirit. Imagine, for a moment, that we can become the subjects of our own masterpiece, a symphony of sighs and moans, a tapestry of lust and longing, a fresco painted with the strokes of our bodies as we succumb to the ecstasy that awaits us."

Michael's breath caught, the air between them now hyper-charged with an undeniable mutual attraction. Marco's eyes held him captive as he spoke. "As we embrace the pleasures of *Venezia*, let us also embrace the truth that lies within us, the truth that we are creatures of desire, longing to be touched, to be tasted, to be consumed by the fire that burns within our souls."

"And now," Marco finished, his voice a seductive

whisper, "invite your curiosity, allow yourself to dive into the abyss of the unknown, and emerge reborn, forever changed by the magic and the passion that is *Venezia*."

The intensity of the moment left Michael breathless. Their eyes remained locked, and for a moment, time seemed to stand still. The world around them faded into the background, and all that existed was the charged air between them, filled with the promise of what could be.

As the music from the café swelled, carrying them deeper into the magic of the moment, the mutual attraction between Michael and Marco became undeniable. The atmosphere was electric, and both men felt the pull of the city's seductive charm, drawing them together in an unspoken promise of adventure and discovery.

Their gazes held, and for the first time in a long while, Michael felt truly alive, ready to embrace whatever *Venezia* had in store for him. The future was uncertain, but in this moment, surrounded by the timeless beauty of Venice and the captivating presence of Marco, he was willing to dive into the unknown and see where the current took him.

Chapter 21

Michael stood nervously with Marco by his side as they approached the table where Liza, Dave, and Anna were sitting. The friends looked up from their drinks, curiosity evident in their eyes.

Anna, feigning surprise, said, "Oh, hi! We didn't see you here!"

Michael cleared his throat, trying to mask his nerves. "Guys, I'd like you to meet Marco. Marco, these are my friends – Liza, Dave, and Anna."

Marco smiled warmly. "It's a pleasure to meet you all."

Liza grinned, her eyes twinkling with mischief. "The pleasure is ours, I'm sure."

Anna extended a hand for a handshake. "Hello, Marco."

Dave, eyeing Marco cautiously, extended his hand as well. "Dave," he said, his tone neutral.

Marco shook Dave's hand firmly. "Nice to meet you, Dave."

"So, Marco, what exactly is it that you do?" Dave asked, his curiosity getting the better of him.

Marco smiled. "I'm a calligraphy instructor."

Michael, eager to steer the conversation, jumped in.

"Marco's going to play tour guide, so we'll see you—"

Dave cut him off enthusiastically. "That's a great idea! We'd love a local to show us around!"

Michael tried to protest, but Liza quickly chimed in. "A private guide, how fantastic!"

Anna added, smiling, "That sounds lovely."

Marco beamed, clearly pleased with the turn of events. "It would be a pleasure to show you all the hidden treasures of Venice."

Michael hesitated, feeling a bit overwhelmed, but didn't object. "Um, cool," he said, trying to muster enthusiasm.

Liza, sensing Michael's apprehension, gave him a reassuring smile. "This is going to be so much fun," she said. "I've always wanted a local's perspective on Venice."

Dave, still cautious but more relaxed, nodded. "Yeah, it'll be good to have someone who knows the city."

Marco, sensing the group's excitement, started to outline a plan. "We can start with some of the lesser-known canals and squares, places that aren't packed with tourists. There are some beautiful spots that even many Venetians don't know about."

As Marco spoke, Michael started to relax. The warmth and confidence in Marco's voice reassured him, and he began to look forward to the day ahead. His friends' acceptance of Marco and their enthusiasm for the tour made him feel more at ease.

"That sounds amazing," Anna said. "I can't wait to see these hidden gems."

"Me neither," Liza agreed. "Lead the way, Marco."

Michael took a deep breath, feeling a sense of relief. "Thanks, Marco," he said, his smile more genuine now.

"I really appreciate this."

Marco placed a hand on Michael's shoulder, giving it a gentle squeeze. "It's my pleasure, Michael. Let's make this a day to remember."

With their plans set, the group finished their drinks and prepared to embark on their adventure. As they stepped out of the café, the sun shining down on them, Michael felt a renewed sense of optimism. The day ahead promised new experiences and the chance to see Venice through Marco's eyes.

Chapter 22

Marco led the group through a maze of narrow alleys, guiding them away from the bustling tourist areas and into the heart of the authentic Venetian experience. The alleys were quiet, lined with ancient buildings and adorned with hanging flower baskets that added a touch of color to the rustic scenery.

"Have you had any *cicchetti*?" Marco asked, grinning as he walked slightly ahead of the group.

Anna looked intrigued. "*Cicchetti?*"

Marco nodded. "*Cicchetti* are small bites, similar to Spanish tapas."

"Oh, not yet," Michael replied, his interest piqued.

Dave continued to eye Marco suspiciously but followed along.

Marco turned to the group, switching to Italian. "*Venite*," he said with a welcoming gesture. "Come."

They followed him through the winding streets until they reached a small, unassuming place that looked like a hidden gem among the city's many eateries.

Marco led them to a quaint *cicchetti* bar, *El Sbarlefo*, its exterior modest and inviting. The charm of the place was evident from the moment they stepped inside.

The friends found a table and sat down, the

atmosphere cozy and intimate. The bar was decorated with rustic wooden furniture and vintage posters, giving it an old-world charm that felt quintessentially Venetian.

Marco, excited to share this local delicacy with his new friends, said, "Their spicy olives are extraordinary."

Michael nodded eagerly. "Let's get some."

Marco ordered an assortment for everyone, speaking fluently with the bartender. The group watched as a variety of *cicchetti* were prepared, each dish looking more appetizing than the last.

Liza glanced around, taking in the ambiance. "This place is so charming. I love that it's off the beaten path."

Anna nodded in agreement. "It definitely feels more authentic."

The food arrived, and Marco helped distribute the plates. The table was soon filled with a colorful array of spicy marinated olives, *crostini* topped with fresh ingredients, and other delightful small bites. The friends were amazed by the variety and presentation, reminiscent of a scene from "Chef's Table."

Dave took a tentative bite of one of the crostini. "Okay, I have to admit, this is delicious," he said, his previous suspicion beginning to melt away.

Despite his lingering caution, even Dave couldn't help but appreciate the charm and authenticity of the experience. The atmosphere of the *cicchetti* bar, combined with the delicious food, began to work its magic on the group.

Marco and Michael found themselves sitting closer together. As they shared the food and conversation, Marco placed his hand on Michael's thigh under the table. Michael was momentarily taken aback, not used to public displays of affection. But the touch was gentle and reassuring, and he relaxed into it.

They exchanged a sincere look, and Michael's heart raced. The connection between them felt electric, the chemistry undeniable. The warmth of Marco's hand on his thigh was both comforting and thrilling, a silent promise of more to come.

The group continued to enjoy their meal, the conversation flowing easily. Marco's knowledge of Venice and his passion for its hidden gems made the experience even more special. As they shared stories and laughter, the bond between them strengthened, turning this simple outing into a memorable adventure.

As the afternoon light filtered through the bar's windows, casting a warm glow over the table, Michael felt a deep sense of contentment. The combination of good food, great company, and the budding romance with Marco made him realize that this trip was everything he had hoped for and more.

Marco, noticing Michael's reflective smile, leaned in closer. "What are you thinking about?" he asked softly.

Michael looked into Marco's eyes, feeling a surge of affection. "Just how perfect this moment is," he replied. "Thank you for showing us this place."

"It's my pleasure, Michael," Marco said, his voice filled with sincerity. "There's so much more to explore. This is just the beginning."

As the group continued to enjoy their *cicchetti* and wine, Michael felt a growing excitement for the adventures that lay ahead. The day, filled with unexpected delights and new connections, had only just begun.

Chapter 23

After a long day of exploring, Marco and Michael found themselves outside the hotel, slightly apart from the rest of the group. The evening air was cool, a gentle breeze carrying the distant sounds of Venice's canals, while the streets were quiet, bathed in the soft glow of street lamps. The sky above was a deep indigo, dotted with the first stars of the night.

Michael took a deep breath, savoring the tranquility of the moment. "Marco," he began sincerely, "I just wanted to say thank you for showing us around today. We had an amazing time."

Marco smiled warmly, his eyes reflecting the dim light. "It was my pleasure, Michael."

They stood close, the air between them charged with unspoken emotions. Michael's eyes met Marco's, and he felt a magnetic pull, drawing him closer. Slowly, he leaned in for a kiss, his heart pounding in anticipation. But Marco gently turned away, a soft smile playing on his lips, not wanting to rush into anything.

"I've had a wonderful time," Marco said softly, his voice a soothing melody. "But it's best if we take things slowly. I'm a bit old-fashioned that way."

Michael nodded, a flicker of disappointment crossing his face. "I understand," he replied, his voice tinged with a mix of respect and regret.

They rejoined the group, the moment between them lingering in the air like a delicate perfume. Marco said his goodbyes, his presence leaving a lasting impression on everyone.

"I hope to see you all again soon," Marco said, his eyes scanning the group with genuine warmth. "Maybe we can continue our adventure tomorrow?"

Liza, always enthusiastic, grinned widely. "Looking forward to it."

Anna nodded in agreement. "Absolutely!"

Even Dave, who had been cautious and reserved, seemed to be warming up. "Yeah," he added, his tone less guarded.

Michael smiled, feeling a connection that went beyond words. "I'd love that. See you tomorrow."

Marco stepped closer to Michael, his breath warm against Michael's ear as he whispered, "Sweet dreams." He kissed Michael's cheek, a brief yet tender gesture that sent a shiver down Michael's spine.

Michael stuttered slightly, his heart racing. "Sweet dreams."

Marco waved, his voice a gentle caress. "Buona notte."

As Marco walked away, his silhouette gradually fading into the labyrinthine streets of Venice, the friends headed inside the hotel. Each of them was lost in their thoughts, reflecting on the day's events and the connections that had begun to form.

Michael lingered outside, his gaze fixed on Marco until he disappeared into the shadows. The night seemed to hold its breath, the city's ancient charm whispering promises of new beginnings and uncharted adventures. The warmth of Marco's kiss still tingled on his cheek, a reminder of the delicate dance they had begun.

With a deep breath, Michael turned towards the hotel, feeling a mix of anticipation and contentment. He knew that tomorrow held the promise of more discoveries, both in the city and within himself. As he entered the hotel, the echoes of the day's laughter and shared moments filled his mind, and he felt a sense of hope blooming in his heart. Venice, with its enchanting beauty and hidden secrets, was weaving its magic around him, and he was ready to embrace whatever came next.

Chapter 24

In a cozy corner of the hotel bar, the warm glow of candlelight flickered off the polished wood and plush seating, creating an inviting and intimate atmosphere. The friends nursed their nightcaps, each lost in their own thoughts about the day's adventures.

Liza broke the comfortable silence with a playful smile. "I have to say, Michael, he's a total catch."

Anna, sipping her wine, nodded enthusiastically. "Absolutely. He's charming, knowledgeable, and did you see how he navigates those narrow streets? It's like he knows every corner of this city."

Michael smiled, a little embarrassed by the attention. His mind drifted back to the way Marco's hand had felt on his cheek, the soft whisper of "sweet dreams" still echoing in his ears. He took a slow sip of his drink, savoring the warmth that spread through him, not just from the alcohol but from the memory of Marco's touch.

Dave, however, wasn't so easily convinced. His brow furrowed, and he leaned forward, his voice stern. "I still don't trust him. There's something off about him. I don't know if it's his charm or his good looks, but it's all too perfect. It's like he's hiding something."

Liza rolled her eyes, her playful demeanor unshaken.

"Oh, Dave. You always think someone's hiding something."

Dave's tone turned defensive. "We barely know the guy. How do we know he's not playing some kind of game with us?"

Anna shook her head, her expression firm. "He was nothing but kind all day. He showed us the best parts of the city, and he did it with a smile. I think that counts for something."

Michael, feeling the need to defend his new friend, chimed in softly. "I think he's nice. He didn't have to spend his day with us, but he did."

Liza, always the romantic, sighed dramatically. "And he's so handsome."

Anna, her eyes dreamy, added, "Oh my god, so handsome..."

The conversation flowed around the table as they finished their drinks. The bar was quiet except for the low hum of their voices and the occasional clink of glassware. The camaraderie among the friends was palpable, each adding their own perspective to the mix. Some were enamored with Marco, enchanted by his charm and good looks, while others remained suspicious, their caution a protective shield against the unknown.

As the night wore on, the group continued to share their thoughts about Marco, their voices a mix of admiration and skepticism. Michael listened, absorbing their words but also holding onto his own experiences and feelings. He appreciated their concern but felt a connection with Marco that he couldn't easily dismiss.

Eventually, the conversation began to wind down. The soft strains of a piano playing in the background added a soothing quality to the atmosphere, encouraging a sense of relaxation and introspection. The bar staff moved quietly, preparing to close for the night, the gentle clinking of glasses and muted footsteps blending into the ambient noise.

Michael stood up, feeling the pleasant buzz of the evening's drinks. He stretched, his muscles relaxing after a long day of exploration and emotional highs. "I think I'm going to head up to bed," he announced, his voice carrying a note of contentment.

His friends nodded in agreement, each of them feeling the pull of sleep after their eventful day. "Goodnight, Michael," Liza said warmly, giving him a knowing smile.

"Sweet dreams," Anna added, echoing Marco's earlier words.

Dave, still looking a bit wary but less tense, offered a nod. "Night, Michael. Sleep well."

Michael made his way out of the bar and up the grand staircase to his room. The plush carpet muffled his footsteps, and the elegant decor of the hotel offered a sense of luxury and comfort. As he reached his room, he paused for a moment, reflecting on the day and the new connections he was forming.

Michael stepped out of the shower, his toned body glistening with droplets of water. He grabbed a towel and began to dry himself off before slipping between the sheets of his bed. The quiet and calm of his room welcomed him as he undressed, the soft sheets cradling him in their warmth.

As he lay there, his thoughts drifted back to Marco—the way his smile lit up his face, the gentle touch of his hand, and the promise of more adventures to come. His gaze, adrift in the sea of memories, lingered upon the day's unfolding narrative.

With a deep breath, Michael closed his eyes, a sense of peace washing over him. The excitement of tomorrow's possibilities mingled with the comfort of the present moment. The city of Venice, with all its beauty and mystery, held endless opportunities for discovery and connection. As he drifted off to sleep, Michael knew that whatever the future held, he was ready to embrace it with an open heart.

Chapter 25

The group sat together at a table in the hotel's breakfast room, surrounded by the sumptuous spread of the morning buffet. The air was filled with the inviting aroma of freshly brewed coffee, warm pastries, and a variety of delectable breakfast options. The table was adorned with an assortment of croissants, cheeses, and various cured meats, each bite promising a burst of flavor. Fresh fruit, yogurt, and granola were artfully arranged, offering a balance to the more indulgent choices. The soft hum of conversation and the clinking of cutlery created a lively yet relaxed atmosphere, perfect for starting the day.

Liza, always the playful one, couldn't resist teasing Michael as she took a sip of her cappuccino. "So, Michael, no late-night rendezvous with Marco after we all went to bed?" she asked, her eyes twinkling with mischief.

Michael shook his head, a small smile playing on his lips as he reached for a golden, buttery croissant. "No, nothing like that."

Liza raised an eyebrow, clearly intrigued. "He didn't come back?"

Michael's expression softened, a hint of amusement in his eyes. "Nope."

Anna, always the inquisitive one, looked genuinely surprised. "Really? That's not like you, Michael."

Dave, his fork poised over a slice of melon, couldn't help but voice his suspicion. "I told you, there's something off about this guy."

Liza scoffed, rolling her eyes as she spread some rich, creamy butter on her toast. "Or maybe he's just a gentleman, Dave. Not everyone jumps into bed on the first date."

Michael, feeling a bit defensive, took a sip of his orange juice. "Hey, I don't always do that, either."

Anna side-eyed Michael, a playful smile tugging at her lips. "It's still a little unusual for you, especially considering how much chemistry you two seem to have."

Michael sighed, leaning back in his chair as he contemplated his friends' words. "I don't know. Maybe he's just old-fashioned. And maybe I should try taking things slow for once."

Liza, ever the romantic, found the idea appealing. "That's kind of refreshing, isn't it? I mean, in this day and age, it's rare to find someone who wants to take their time and actually get to know you."

Dave, still not convinced, narrowed his eyes slightly as he pushed his plate aside. "Or maybe he's playing some kind of game. Who turns down a good-looking sexpot like Michael?"

Michael couldn't help but laugh at Dave's bluntness, though he appreciated the compliment. "I appreciate that he didn't just want to jump into bed with me. Sure, I was disappointed, but I was also eager to explore more than just his body."

The conversation continued, punctuated by laughter and the enjoyment of their delicious breakfast. The pastries were perfectly flaky, the fruit was fresh and sweet, and the coffee was strong and invigorating. It was a meal that nourished both body and soul, setting the tone for the adventures that lay ahead. As they chatted and enjoyed the sumptuous spread, the bond between them grew stronger, each moment shared adding another layer to their friendship.

Chapter 26

The next day dawned with a mix of excitement and anticipation for Michael. The sun was shining, casting long, golden rays through the narrow streets of Venice, but there was an undercurrent of unease that Michael couldn't quite shake. He made his way through the labyrinthine alleyways, his heart pounding with the thrill of seeing Marco again. Each step seemed to echo his growing excitement, but there was a shadow lingering in the back of his mind.

As he turned a corner, Michael's heart nearly stopped. Standing there, like a dark specter from his past, was Angelo, the sexy Italian man Michael had given a blowjob to earlier. Angelo's eyes locked onto Michael's with an intensity that sent a shiver down his spine.

"Hey, you want to fuck?" Angelo asked in Italian, his voice low and suggestive.

Michael's pulse quickened, a mix of fear and anger rising within him. Angelo grabbed his own bulge, licking his lips in a lewd display, and motioned for Michael to follow him. The narrow street suddenly felt even more confined, the buildings closing in like a trap.

"No," Michael said firmly, shaking his head. He tried to keep his voice steady, but the fear was evident.

Angelo was persistent. He followed Michael,

continuing to speak temptingly in Italian. The words were foreign to Michael, but the tone was unmistakable. Each syllable dripped with a predatory hunger. Angelo's presence was suffocating, like a dark cloud hanging over Michael's every step.

The streets seemed to narrow even more as Michael quickened his pace. Angelo's footsteps echoed behind him, a constant reminder that he wasn't alone. Suddenly, Angelo reached out and grabbed Michael's bulge. The touch was aggressive, invasive. Michael's anger flared, and he quickly slapped Angelo's hand away.

"I said no!" Michael shouted, his voice echoing off the stone walls. The narrow alley seemed to amplify his fear, the shadows growing longer and darker.

He broke into a near-run, his breath coming in short, panicked bursts. Angelo continued to follow him, his presence like a dark shadow that refused to be shaken off. Michael turned a corner, glancing back over his shoulder. Angelo was still there, his predatory gaze locked onto Michael.

Another turn, and Michael's heart pounded even harder. He could feel Angelo's eyes on him, feel the oppressive weight of his presence. The narrow streets seemed to twist and turn endlessly, each corner a potential escape that led nowhere.

On the final turn, Michael glanced back once more, his heart in his throat. Angelo had finally stopped following him, his dark figure fading into the distance. Michael's legs felt like jelly, his breath coming in ragged gasps. He leaned against a wall, trying to calm his racing heart.

Breathing a sigh of relief, Michael straightened up and continued toward the meeting spot for his date with

Marco. The excitement and anticipation had been tainted by fear, but the thought of seeing Marco again gave him the strength to keep moving forward. As he walked, the shadows seemed to recede, and the golden light of Venice once again bathed the streets in a warm, welcoming glow.

But the memory of Angelo's touch, the darkness in his eyes, lingered in Michael's mind. The city of Venice, with all its beauty and mystery, held secrets that were both thrilling and terrifying. And as he made his way to Marco, Michael couldn't help but wonder what other shadows might be lurking in the narrow streets of this ancient city.

Chapter 27

Michael arrived at the rendezvous spot, his heart pounding with anticipation. As he scanned the area, his eyes caught sight of Marco approaching in the distance. The excitement and nervousness intermingled within him, creating a palpable tension that coursed through his veins.

As Marco drew nearer, his face lit up with a warm smile. He opened his arms, and Michael stepped into his embrace, feeling the comfort and strength in Marco's hug. The embrace lingered for a moment, both men savoring the closeness.

Marco led Michael inside *Cicchetteria Al Pesce Rosso*, the aroma of freshly ground coffee beans filling the air. The cozy interior was bustling with locals and tourists alike, each savoring their drinks and conversations. Marco greeted Lucia, the owner, with a warm smile.

"Marco, my friend! Come," Lucia said in Italian, her eyes twinkling with familiarity.

"*Grazie*, Lucia! You're always so kind," Marco responded, his tone filled with genuine appreciation.

Lucia invited them to sit at a table by the window, where they could enjoy the view of the canal outside. The sun cast a golden glow over the water, creating a picturesque scene that seemed almost surreal. As they settled into their seats, the atmosphere between them grew more intimate, the bustling café around them fading into the background.

Michael took a deep breath, his fingers tracing the edge of his coffee cup. "Marco, there's something I wanted to share with you," he began, his voice tinged with nervousness. "My last relationship ended quite badly. I was betrayed and abandoned by someone I thought I could trust."

Marco's expression softened with empathy. "Oh, no. I'm so sorry. It's a terrible thing to experience betrayal, especially from someone you love."

Michael nodded, feeling a mixture of relief and vulnerability. "Yes, it is."

Marco reached across the table, gently squeezing Michael's hand. "You are strong. And resilient, for sure. It's good you are opening to new experiences."

Michael looked into Marco's eyes, feeling a connection that went beyond words. "How do you know I am?" he asked, a small smile playing on his lips.

Marco's eyes twinkled with warmth. "Well, for starters, you're sitting in Venice and not locked in your room back home."

As they continued their conversation, the initial nervousness began to fade. Michael subtly inched his leg towards Marco's, gently pressing it against him. The physical connection sent a thrill through them both, the spark of desire igniting between them.

"It's nice getting to know you," Michael whispered, his voice filled with sincerity.

"I feel the same way," Marco whispered back, his gaze locking onto Michael's. The intensity of their eyes spoke volumes, and for a moment, the world around them disappeared.

"When I'm close to you, I feel this intense heat, this passion I haven't felt for ages. It's just... exciting," Michael confessed, his voice trembling with emotion.

Marco's gaze grew more intense, his eyes smoldering with desire. He responded in Italian, his voice low and seductive, *"Desiderio è una forza potente. Trascende il banale, risvegliando i nostri istinti e impulsi più profondi."*

Slowly, Marco moved his hand under the table, brushing against Michael's thigh. The touch was feather-light and electrifying, sending shivers down Michael's spine. He caught his breath, struggling to keep his voice steady.

"I can't stop thinking about getting naked with you," Michael admitted, his voice barely above a whisper.

Marco discreetly reached over to Michael's crotch, hidden beneath the tablecloth, moving his hand firmly against Michael's bulge. *"Godiamoci la magia dell'attesa e lasciamo che le fiamme del desiderio continuino ad ardere,"* Marco whispered seductively.

Michael struggled to maintain his composure, his voice trembling. "I want to feel you..."

Marco's gaze remained locked on Michael's, his voice low and hypnotic as his fingers lightly glided along the curve of Michael's erection. *"Desiderio è una forza potente. Trascende il banale, risvegliando i nostri istinti e impulsi più profondi."*

Michael's breath grew shallow, his body trembling with intensity. Marco continued to massage him, his voice taking on an even more hypnotic quality. *"Quando cediamo ai nostri desideri, permettiamo a noi stessi di sperimentare gli aspetti più primitivi, più crudi e più vulnerabili del nostro essere. È una resa, un rilascio... di controllo... che può portare al piacere più squisito."*

Michael closed his eyes for a moment, surrendering to the sensations of Marco's fingers. Marco's words washed over him, the fire of desire burning hotter within him as he savored the touch of Marco's fingers.

"Desiderio ci ricorda il nostro bisogno innato di intimità, il desiderio fondamentale di essere visti e compresi da qualcun altro. Lasciamo che i nostri desideri ci guidino, godiamoci l'eccitazione, la tentazione e il puro brivido di scoprire i segreti l'uno dell'altro, mentre abbracciamo l'irresistibile fascino di ciò che ci aspetta," Marco continued, his voice a seductive whisper.

Michael's breath grew heavy, his body trembling with need. "I don't... understand... what you're saying but..."

Marco smiled seductively. "Desire has the power to elevate us, to transport us to a realm where pleasure and passion merge, transcending the boundaries of our everyday existence. But, we must also remember to balance our desires with restraint."

Michael gazed deeply into Marco's eyes, his longing for physical connection overwhelming him. "I want to kiss you so badly."

Marco leaned in closer, his smile filled with a mix of desire and restraint. "Yes, this is the sweet pain of desire."

As Marco spoke, his fingers continued to massage and rub Michael's dick under the table, maintaining the sensual tension between them. Marco noticed a small wet spot forming on Michael's pants, at the tip of his erection. With a sly smile, Marco playfully traced the damp area with his finger.

"Desire is not always easily contained," Marco teased.

Michael, too caught up in the sensations to feel embarrassed, simply nodded, his eyes locked on Marco's. "I find that incredibly sexy," Marco continued.

Marco removed his hand from Michael's erection and brought it to his lips, licking the wetness from his fingertips. "Like honey," he said with a sly smile.

Michael couldn't help but laugh a little, the tension easing as they shared a moment of genuine connection and intimacy. Marco laughed too, the sound warm and genuine, filling the small room with a sense of joy and closeness.

"Marco," Michael whispered, his voice filled with longing, "I can't wait to explore this connection with you."

"Soon enough," Marco replied, his eyes filled with promise and desire.

The two men sat there, their hands intertwined under the table, the world outside forgotten as they basked in the warmth of their connection. The promise of what lay ahead filled the air with a sense of excitement and anticipation, as they embraced the undeniable allure of their growing bond.

Chapter 28

Michael and Marco left the café, the quaint charm of the establishment giving way to the labyrinthine alleys of Venice. The air was filled with the rich aroma of freshly brewed coffee, mingling with the faint scent of the nearby canals. The cobblestone streets were lined with historic buildings, their facades adorned with intricate carvings and vibrant flower boxes. The soft murmur of the city, punctuated by the occasional laughter of tourists and the distant calls of *gondoliers*, created a soothing soundtrack to their stroll.

As they walked side by side, Marco brushed his hand against Michael's, their fingers gently intertwining. The simple touch sent a thrill through Michael, the connection between them growing stronger with each passing moment.

"I have a calligraphy student soon and must go," Marco said, his voice tinged with regret. "Will I see you tomorrow?"

Michael's heart sank a little at the thought of parting but lifted again at the prospect of seeing Marco the next day. "Of course," he replied, his voice filled with warmth and anticipation. "Should I..."

Before he could finish, Marco interrupted him with a playful smile. *"Ciao bello,"* he said, his eyes twinkling with affection.

Marco's face lit up at Michael's response, clearly pleased. With a warm smile and a light squeeze of Michael's hand, Marco reluctantly pulled away. "Ci vediamo domani," he added, his voice soft and full of promise.

Michael stood there for a moment, watching Marco walk away. The narrow alley seemed to close in around him, the shadows lengthening as the sun dipped lower in the sky. Despite the impending darkness, Michael felt a lightness in his heart, a sense of hope and excitement for what lay ahead.

The city of Venice, with its winding streets and hidden corners, seemed to hold endless possibilities. As Marco disappeared from sight, Michael turned and continued his walk, the memory of their touch lingering like a soft caress. He knew that tomorrow would bring new adventures, and he was ready to embrace them with an open heart.

Chapter 29

Michael and Liza strolled along the picturesque canal, the gentle sway of *gondolas* creating ripples in the water as they glided smoothly by. The *gondoliers*, dressed in their traditional attire, serenaded couples with romantic songs, their voices mingling with the soft sounds of the city. The air was filled with a blend of aromas – freshly baked pastries from nearby cafes, the earthy scent of the canals, and the subtle hint of blooming flowers from window boxes above.

Locals passed them by, some engaged in animated conversations, others lost in their thoughts. The city's unique charm was palpable, every corner revealing a new story, a hidden treasure. The architecture, a blend of Gothic and Renaissance, stood as a testament to Venice's rich history and enduring beauty.

Michael turned to Liza, his expression sincere. "Do you ever think about your own true desire?" he asked, his voice thoughtful.

Liza looked at him curiously, her brow furrowing slightly. "What do you mean?" she replied, her curiosity piqued.

"I've realized that I crave more than just physical intimacy," Michael continued, his tone contemplative. "Sex is great, don't get me wrong. But I want a deeper connection with someone."

Liza nodded, understanding. "You know, being here... there's like this fleeting vibe. It's a city that seems to be sinking, but it just keeps going. Maybe that's what love is truly all about."

Michael smiled at her words, his mind turning over the idea. "Gorgeous and charming, but also delicate and at the whim of whatever life throws at it," he mused.

"Yeah, totally," Liza agreed, her gaze drifting over the canal. "And even with that fragility, we still chase after it: passion, love. Maybe that's why you're drawn to Marco."

"He's got this passion and charm about him," Michael said, a smile spreading across his face. "But, I can't help but wonder..."

Liza's expression turned sincere, her eyes meeting Michael's. "What he's hiding? That's the beauty of human connection, Michael. We're all a mix of tough and vulnerable. Look at Dave and Anna."

Michael nodded, seeing her point. "I see what you mean."

"It's up to us to navigate those complexities and find the love that endures," Liza continued, her voice filled with conviction.

They walked in silence for a moment, the soft murmur of the canal and the distant sounds of the city providing a soothing backdrop. The scene around them felt almost dreamlike, the light reflecting off the water and casting shimmering patterns on the ancient buildings. It was as if Venice itself was whispering secrets of love and resilience, encouraging them to embrace the journey ahead.

As they continued their walk, Michael felt a sense of

clarity. The city, with its timeless beauty and quiet strength, mirrored the complexities of love he was beginning to understand. He knew that his path with Marco, though uncertain, held the promise of something profound. And with friends like Liza by his side, he felt ready to navigate whatever life had in store.

Michael and Liza sat in a cozy corner of the *cicchetti* bar, the atmosphere warm and inviting. The bar was bustling with life, the clinking of glasses and the soft hum of conversation creating a lively backdrop. The air was filled with the mouthwatering aromas of freshly prepared snacks – bite-sized *cicchetti*, each more tempting than the last. Plates of crostini topped with creamy cod mousse, marinated olives, and prosciutto-wrapped figs were artfully arranged on the table in front of them.

Michael picked up a glass of ruby-red wine, taking a sip as he contemplated the scene around them. "Isn't it fascinating how love can be both our sanctuary and our greatest challenge?" he mused, his voice thoughtful. "I think that's what's made my past relationships so difficult. I was so consumed by the appearance of it all, and yet, never once did I confront the vulnerability and fear."

Liza nodded, her own glass of wine poised at her lips. "Absolutely. The duality of love is what makes it so compelling," she said, her tone equally reflective. "We crave the comfort and security it provides, while simultaneously facing the uncertainty and complexities that come with it. It's a delicate balance, one that requires us to be both resilient and willing to surrender."

She smiled, her eyes twinkling with the light of the bar's softly glowing lanterns. "Love and Venice, both bound by the same intoxicating dance between strength and vulnerability. It's no wonder you found yourself drawn to Marco here of all places."

Michael looked down at his plate, absently picking up a piece of crostini. "And perhaps the fact that he's taking things slowly is an opportunity for us to truly explore the depths of our connection, rather than simply getting swept away by the initial rush of it all," he said, his voice tinged with hope.

Liza reached for a prosciutto-wrapped fig, her smile widening. "Taking the time to build a solid foundation can make all the difference in the long run," she agreed, her eyes meeting Michael's. "A relationship built on a strong foundation can withstand the tests of time and circumstance."

The two friends continued to enjoy their snacks and wine, their conversation weaving between reflections on love and the beauty of their surroundings. The bar's rustic charm, with its exposed wooden beams and flickering candles, provided the perfect setting for such a heartfelt discussion. The wine flowed freely, and as the evening wore on, Michael and Liza found themselves sharing more than just food and drink – they were sharing their hopes, fears, and dreams.

As they talked, Michael felt a sense of clarity emerging from the haze of his emotions. The warmth of the wine, the delicious flavors of the *cicchetti*, and the comfort of Liza's presence all combined to create a moment of genuine connection. He realized that the journey he was on, both with Marco and within himself, was one of discovery and growth.

Liza's words resonated deeply with him. The idea of love as a dance between strength and vulnerability, much like the city of Venice itself, struck a chord. He knew that his past relationships had faltered because he had been afraid to confront his own fears and insecurities. But now, with Marco, he felt a newfound willingness to embrace the uncertainties and complexities that came with love.

As they finished their wine and snacks, the *cicchetti* bar began to quiet down, the patrons gradually making their way home. Michael and Liza lingered for a moment longer, savoring the last sips of their wine and the warmth of their friendship. The evening had been a reminder that, despite the challenges and fears that love presented, it was also a source of immense beauty and joy.

With a contented sigh, Michael set down his empty glass and looked at Liza. "Thanks for this," he said softly. "I needed it."

Liza reached across the table and squeezed his hand. "Anytime, Michael," she replied, her voice filled with affection. "Remember, we're all in this dance together. And sometimes, the best thing we can do is just keep moving, one step at a time."

As they left the bar and stepped back into the cool night air, Michael felt a renewed sense of purpose. The city of Venice, with all its beauty and mystery, seemed to embrace him, urging him to continue his journey with an open heart. And with friends like Liza by his side, he knew that whatever lay ahead, he was ready to face it.

Chapter 30

The warm, golden light of the late afternoon sun filtered through the windows of the quaint bar, casting a cozy glow over the friends as they gathered around a small, rustic table. The ambiance was inviting, with the gentle hum of conversation blending harmoniously with the soft clinking of glasses and the occasional burst of laughter from other patrons. The air was rich with the aroma of aged wood, mingling with the subtle scent of freshly brewed coffee and the lingering notes of various spirits.

Marco sat with a relaxed demeanor, his fingers deftly rubbing grains of salt between his thumb and index finger. He looked thoughtful, a gentle smile playing on his lips. "You know," he began, his voice carrying a melodic warmth, "I've been thinking about how we often judge each other, and the concept of being judgmental. In my opinion, judgment is just a construct; it doesn't really exist."

Dave, always the skeptic, raised an eyebrow, his tone dripping with sarcasm. "Oh really? So you're saying we're all just making it up as we go along, like some kind of mass hallucination?"

Liza, sitting beside him, nodded thoughtfully. "I think there's some truth to that, actually. Like, we're all just projecting our own stuff onto others, right? It's less about the person we're judging and more about what's going on in our own heads."

Marco's smile widened, clearly pleased with her understanding. "Exactly. If we can step back and recognize that, we can open ourselves up to more genuine connections and understanding, instead of letting judgment cloud our view of others."

He leaned back in his chair, his eyes taking on a reflective sheen. "You know, this idea of judgment and constructs leads me to another thought – that there's no such thing as good or bad, or right or wrong. It reminds me of something Alan Watts, or somebody, once said. That in the grand scheme of the universe, the only thing that exists is what IS, and whatever that IS, it's neither good nor bad, nor right nor wrong. It simply IS."

Dave looked intrigued, but not entirely convinced. "How so?"

Marco turned to face the group, his gaze earnest. "It's easy to get caught up in our own subjective experiences and categorize everything into these dualities. But if we step back, beyond our personal judgments and perceptions, we can see that the world, the universe, and everything in it are interconnected and constantly changing."

He smiled, his words flowing with a poetic grace. "It's a dance of existence, a cosmic ballet where each element is part of a bigger picture. By letting go of these arbitrary labels we've created, we can appreciate the beauty and complexity of life as it is. In that perspective, there's no need to cling to these polarizing notions of good and bad or right and wrong. We can simply be present, experiencing each moment fully and with openness, embracing the infinite dance that is the essence of being."

Dave leaned forward, his expression challenging but curious. "Hold on a second, Marco. If there's no inherent good or bad, or right or wrong, how do we make decisions? Or, how do we differentiate between acts that cause harm and those that promote well-being? Aren't there some universally agreed-upon moral standards that help guide us in making choices? I mean, there's got to be some foundation to morality, right?"

Marco's smile remained patient as he addressed Dave's concerns. "Dave, I understand your concerns, but let's consider the etymology and history of the word 'morality.' It has its origins in religious doctrine and was shaped by the Church to impose certain values and beliefs. Before the development of religious institutions as we know them, there were different ways in which societies understood and approached the concepts of right and wrong."

At that moment, the waiter arrived with another round of drinks, the glasses clinking softly as they were set down on the table. Michael took a sip of his drink, nodding thoughtfully. "Totally. And, while it's true that people have always had a sense of ethics and social responsibility, the idea of a singular, objective standard of right and wrong didn't always exist."

Dave sighed, a hint of frustration in his voice. "Blame the church."

Marco nodded, his eyes reflecting a deep understanding. "When I say there's no inherent good or bad, or right or wrong, I'm suggesting that our perceptions of these concepts are fluid and subjective, depending on the cultural and personal lenses through which we view the world. The challenge lies in recognizing and appreciating this diversity of perspectives and finding ways to coexist harmoniously, even when our values and beliefs differ."

Liza leaned in, her enthusiasm evident. "Exactly! Our judgments are shaped by our personal experiences and the values we've been taught. When we label something as 'good' or 'bad,' we're often projecting our own beliefs and expectations onto the situation, instead of simply observing it as it is."

Michael nodded in agreement, his voice thoughtful. "I am as I am."

Dave, still skeptical, pressed on. "But what about murderers? Are you saying they aren't bad? How can you not judge something as evil when it causes so much suffering?"

Marco remained calm, his voice steady. "Dave, let me give you a different perspective. When a lion kills a goat for dinner, we don't consider the lion evil or a murderer; we understand that it's just a lion being a lion. It's part of the natural order, and the lion is just following its instincts to survive. It simply is what it is."

Dave frowned, trying to wrap his mind around the concept. "But murderers as in people?"

Marco's expression softened, his tone empathetic. "I'm not condoning monstrous acts committed by people, but my point is that labeling someone as 'bad' or 'evil' doesn't solve the problem or help us understand the underlying issues that drive such behavior. We must examine the complex factors and circumstances that contribute to those actions. In doing so, we can work towards addressing the root causes and creating a more compassionate and empathetic society, rather than merely labeling and condemning individuals based on our own subjective moral judgments."

Michael leaned in, intrigued by the conversation. "So, if we follow that line of thinking, even something like pornography could be considered a construct, right? I mean, it's only seen as 'bad' or 'taboo' because of the way society perceives it."

Dave raised an eyebrow, still doubtful. "I think that's a stretch."

Marco smiled, appreciating Michael's insight. "Well, actually, Michael has a point. Just like our moral judgments, our perception of what constitutes pornography is shaped by cultural and societal values. If you look at nature and the animal kingdom, mating and reproduction are natural parts of life. There is no 'shame' or 'taboo' attached to these acts in the wild."

Liza laughed, adding her own perspective. "Agreed. If two birds are having sex on a branch, and another bird sees, that bird isn't thinking, 'How offensive, get a room.'"

Marco chuckled, nodding. "Yes, in a way, what we label as pornography could also be seen as a construct created by human judgment and societal norms. It doesn't mean we should completely disregard the potential negative aspects associated with it, but it's essential to recognize that our perception of it is highly influenced by the lens through which we view the world."

Michael added, his voice contemplative. "What might be considered inappropriate or offensive in one culture could be entirely acceptable or even revered in another. For instance, some tribal societies in Africa and South America consider nudity and body decorations as natural expressions of their culture and a way of life."

Liza nodded in agreement. "There are tons of examples of things that were once considered pornographic that aren't now. Take the Victorian era, where even showing your ankles was scandalous."

Marco smiled, the conversation energizing him. "And, during the Renaissance, works of art that depicted nudity or sensual themes, such as Botticelli's 'The Birth of Venus' or Michelangelo's 'David,' were often criticized and censored. Today, we view these masterpieces as timeless expressions of human beauty and creativity."

Michael sighed contentedly. "God, I love evolution."

Marco continued, his voice thoughtful. "So, now you see, the concept of what is pornographic or taboo changes across cultures and throughout history. These variations further support the idea that our judgments are merely constructs shaped by societal values and beliefs, rather than absolute truths."

Liza leaned back, her eyes sparkling with interest. "I remember when I was a kid, even the slightest hint of nudity on TV would cause an uproar. But now, there's full-on sex in several major shows, and it's considered completely normal."

Marco nodded, his smile widening. "And even artistic."

Dave, finally joining in with a hint of amusement, added, "Yeah, like the rimming scene in 'White Lotus.'"

Michael rolled his eyes playfully, a smile tugging at his lips. "It just goes to show that our perceptions and standards change over time."

Liza sighed, a sense of wonder in her voice. "It's fascinating."

The group fell into a thoughtful silence, each of them sipping their drinks and reflecting on the conversation.

Marco's voice broke the silence, his tone gentle but firm. "Exactly, my friends. When we, as a species, can finally eliminate judgment from our beings, we will have come a long way. It's about embracing the ever-changing nature of our understanding and allowing ourselves to grow and evolve without being constrained by outdated concepts of what is right or wrong. Only then can we truly appreciate the full spectrum of human experiences and the beautiful complexity of life itself."

As the conversation wound down, the friends shared a moment of quiet contemplation, the warmth of their connection filling the space between them. The bar around them hummed with life, but in that moment, Michael and Marco shared an intimate exchange of looks, it felt as they were the only ones there. The ambient noise of clinking glasses, soft laughter, and the murmur of conversations faded into the background, creating a bubble of connection that enveloped them.

As the night wound down and the group began to part ways, Michael and Marco found themselves alone, sharing a quiet moment together. Marco turned to the group, his voice filled with warmth and gratitude. *"Bella gente! È stata una grande serata,"* he said, his eyes shining with genuine affection.

Anna, feeling the effects of the evening's drinks, giggled and replied playfully, "We love you, Marco!" Her voice carried a hint of a slur, but her sentiment was clear.

Marco turned to Michael, his expression softening. "I must go and prepare for work now," he said, his voice low and intimate. "I will see you tomorrow. But for now, let us meet again in our dreams."

They shared a tight embrace, their bodies pressed close together, their hearts beating in harmony as they held each other. The embrace lasted longer than seven seconds, each moment stretching into an eternity of shared warmth and connection.

Slowly, they parted, their eyes lingering on one another. Marco gently cupped Michael's face in his hands, his touch tender and reassuring. He leaned in and pressed a soft, lingering kiss on Michael's forehead, a gesture filled with unspoken promises and affection.

"Sweet dreams, Michael," Marco whispered, his breath warm against Michael's skin.

With a final, lingering look, Marco turned to leave. Michael watched him go, his heart swelling with hope and anticipation for what the future might hold. The memory of Marco's touch and the warmth of his embrace stayed with him, a comforting reminder of the connection they shared. As Marco disappeared into the night, Michael felt a sense of peace and excitement, ready to embrace whatever tomorrow might bring.

Chapter 31

Michael and Marco explored the enchanting city of Venice, their love story unfolding like a beautiful postcard, each scene bathed in the city's romantic glow.

They sat together at a quaint outdoor café, sipping on vibrant Aperol Spritzes. The sunlight filtered through the leaves of nearby trees, casting dappled shadows on their faces as they laughed and toasted to their new adventures. Michael's eyes sparkled with joy as Marco leaned in close, whispering something that made him blush and smile.

Later, they shared a creamy gelato, the rich flavors melting on their tongues. Michael, ever the tease, turned the act of licking the gelato into something playful and suggestive, his eyes filled with mischief. Marco laughed, playfully pushing Michael's face away, insisting with a grin, "Not everything is sexual, Michael!" The air filled with their laughter, the sweetness of the gelato mirrored in their shared joy.

They strolled through bustling markets, sampling *cicchetti* snacks from street vendors. The small bites of Venetian tapas brought delight to their faces as they fed each other, the intimacy of the moment deepening their connection. Their fingers brushed and intertwined, a silent promise of affection and companionship.

Walking along a serene canal, they held hands, their fingers laced together as they navigated the narrow, winding streets. The *gondolas* glided by, the gentle swish of the water creating a soothing backdrop to their whispered conversations and stolen glances.

One rainy afternoon, they found themselves under a shared umbrella, the raindrops creating a soft symphony around them. They stopped in a quiet alleyway, their faces close, the umbrella shielding them from the world. Marco pulled Michael in for a kiss, their lips meeting with a tender intensity, the rain adding a layer of magic to the moment.

Inside the Guggenheim, they marveled at the modern art, their fingers lightly touching as they discussed the pieces. The vibrant colors and bold shapes of the art reflected in their eyes, their shared appreciation for beauty deepening their bond. Michael pointed out a particular sculpture, his excitement palpable, and Marco listened intently, his gaze soft and affectionate.

In the *Basilica San Marco*, Michael stood in awe of the gold mosaic tiles that covered the interior. The grandeur of the church and the intricate details of the mosaics left him speechless. Marco watched him, a soft smile on his lips, appreciating the wonder and reverence in Michael's eyes. They shared a quiet moment of reflection, the sacred space amplifying their connection.

A boat ride took them to Murano, where they watched a master glassblower at work. The fire roared, the heat palpable as the glassblower expertly manipulated the molten glass. He shaped a small vase, his hands moving with precision and skill. Michael and Marco stood close together, their faces illuminated by the glow of the furnace. The glassblower rolled the molten glass on the marver, then inflated it with a long blowpipe, creating a delicate bubble. He spun and shaped the bubble, the colors swirling within the glass like a captured rainbow. The master craftsman used various tools to pinch and pull the glass into a graceful vase, the final product a testament to his artistry.

Michael and Marco exchanged glances, their appreciation for the beauty of the moment evident. The process, from the intense heat to the delicate creation, mirrored their own relationship—born from passion and molded by tenderness.

They walked hand in hand along the Rialto Bridge, the iconic structure offering breathtaking views of the Grand Canal. They stopped to admire the view, the city's lights reflecting off the water like shimmering stars. Marco wrapped an arm around Michael, pulling him close, their hearts beating in harmony as they held each other, soaking in the timeless beauty of Venice.

Chapter 32

The group sat around a table laden with fresh pastries, succulent fruits, and steaming cups of strong Venetian coffee. The scent of freshly baked goods mingled with the robust aroma of the coffee, creating an inviting and comforting atmosphere. The morning light filtered through the window, casting a warm glow over their faces.

Dave sighed, taking a sip of his coffee. "I can't believe this is our last day in Venice. I'm really going to miss this place."

Liza, ever the playful one, teased him. "That's a surprise. Lucky for me, I still have a few more days to explore and..." Her voice trailed off as a sexy Italian woman sitting nearby caught her eye. Liza returned the woman's flirtatious gaze with a mischievous smile. "...soak up all the Venetian charm I can."

Anna smiled, her eyes twinkling with the same warmth as the sun streaming through the window. "We'll have to plan another friends trip again sometime."

Dave's sarcasm cut through the sentimental moment. "Oh? And who's paying for it? You know how expensive this place is?" Everyone chuckled, the shared laughter lightening the bittersweet mood.

Liza, always curious and never one to miss a chance

to tease, shot a knowing glance at Michael. "So, Michael, I can't help but wonder... Is Marco a good kisser?"

The table fell silent, everyone's eyes on Michael. He hesitated, feeling the weight of their anticipation. "Well, actually... we haven't even made out yet."

Liza's fork slipped from her fingers, clanking loudly against her plate. Everyone stared at Michael in shock.

Anna was the first to break the silence. "Really? You?"

Dave raised an eyebrow, his voice dripping with disbelief. "Yeah, I thought you would've at least gotten each other pregnant by now."

Liza burst out laughing, patting Dave on the back. "Dave, you're too much."

Michael sighed deeply, his gaze dropping to his coffee cup. "You know, guys, as much as I appreciate the slow pace and the buildup, I have to admit that it's driving me a bit crazy." He paused, his voice wavering. "What if he isn't attracted to me?"

His friends exchanged concerned looks, their hearts aching for Michael. Anna reached out, placing a comforting hand on his arm. "Oh, sweetie, I highly doubt that's the case. The way he looks at you... There's definitely a strong connection there."

Liza nodded in agreement, her expression serious for once. "Absolutely. I've seen the way he interacts with you. There's a genuine chemistry, no doubt."

Dave leaned forward, trying to offer support in his own way. "Yeah, don't overthink it, Mikey. Just enjoy the ride and let things happen naturally."

Michael took a deep breath, feeling a bit more reassured. "Thanks, guys. I really appreciate it."

Dave, always the pragmatic one, added, "Maybe you should just confront him. Be open and honest about how you feel. It's not like you live here, and time is limited."

Michael considered Dave's words, a mixture of hope and anxiety swirling in his chest. He looked around at his friends, their faces filled with encouragement and support. The shared meal, the laughter, and the heartfelt conversation made him realize just how lucky he was to have such wonderful people in his life.

As the morning passed, they continued to chat and savor the delicious breakfast. The bonds of friendship felt stronger than ever, and despite the uncertainties and challenges ahead, Michael knew he had a solid foundation of love and support to lean on.

Chapter 33

Michael sat in his hotel room, the soft glow of his laptop screen illuminating his face as he gazed out the window over the Grand Canal. The city of Venice lay before him, its beauty both captivating and overwhelming. The gentle ripple of the water and the distant hum of life outside served as a calming backdrop to his conversation with Dr. Gika on Zoom.

Dr. Gika's warm smile filled the screen, her presence a comforting balm for Michael's troubled thoughts. "Michael, it's important to remember that vulnerability is a natural part of any relationship. Opening ourselves up to others always comes with the risk of getting hurt, but it's also what allows us to experience deep connections and joy."

Michael sighed, his eyes shifting from the laptop to the picturesque scene outside. "I know, but with Marco... it's just so different." He paused, searching for the right words. "We've been taking things slow, and I appreciate that, but it's driving me crazy not knowing where we stand. What if he doesn't feel the same way about me?"

Dr. Gika nodded, her expression understanding and empathetic. "It's normal to have doubts and insecurities. But it's also important to communicate openly and honestly with Marco. Share your feelings with him and ask him about his thoughts and intentions. This way, you both can work towards creating a shared understanding and navigate this journey together."

Michael nodded, feeling a mixture of anxiety and determination. "You're right. I need to talk to him about it. I just don't want to scare him away or come across as too needy."

"It's not needy to express your feelings and desires, Michael," Dr. Gika reassured him. "That's a crucial aspect of building a strong, intimate relationship. Be honest and open about your feelings, and trust in the connection that you share with Marco. And remember, no matter what the outcome, you will learn and grow from this experience."

Michael took a deep breath, feeling a sense of relief wash over him. He knew he needed to have that conversation with Marco, but hearing it from Dr. Gika gave him the push he needed. "Okay," he said, his voice steadier.

Dr. Gika's smile widened, a look of genuine pride in her eyes. "Take a moment and connect with your inner voice. It's that powerful, authentic part of yourself that knows what you truly want and need. When we nurture and listen to that voice, we can build trust in ourselves and in our ability to make decisions that are true for us. Reflect on your emotions, desires, and values."

Michael closed his eyes for a moment, letting her words sink in. The sounds of Venice—*gondolas* gliding through the canals, the distant chatter of tourists, the occasional call of a street vendor—blended into a soothing symphony that helped him center himself.

"The key is to be patient and kind with yourself as you learn to connect with your inner voice. As you practice, you'll develop a stronger sense of self-awareness and self-trust," Dr. Gika continued.

Michael opened his eyes, a newfound sense of determination in his gaze. "Okay," he said again, more resolutely this time.

"Remember, Michael, trusting in yourself is crucial for building healthy, loving relationships. When we know ourselves and our worth, we can better communicate our needs, set boundaries, and make choices that are aligned with our true desires."

With a newfound sense of self-assurance, Michael felt more confident. He thanked Dr. Gika, and as he ended the call, he felt a weight lift off his shoulders. The conversation had given him the clarity he needed. He looked out over the Grand Canal once more, feeling a deep sense of peace and readiness to embrace whatever came next.

The city of Venice, with its endless possibilities and hidden wonders, seemed to reflect his own journey of discovery and growth. As he sat there, absorbing the beauty and tranquility of the scene before him, he knew he was ready to take the next step with Marco. Whatever the outcome, he was confident in his ability to navigate the complexities of love and connection, guided by his inner voice and newfound self-awareness.

Chapter 34

Libreria Acqua Alta, the world's most famous bookstore, lived up to its name in every possible way. Nestled in a quiet corner of Venice, the bookstore was a treasure trove of literary wonders. Books were stacked haphazardly from floor to ceiling, creating an enchanting labyrinth. A giant *gondola* sat in the middle of the store, filled to the brim with volumes of all shapes and sizes, a testament to the city's history with the ever-present threat of flooding. The bookstore, with its quirky decor and unique charm, had become a symbol of resilience and creativity, drawing book lovers from all corners of the globe.

Michael and Marco wandered through the maze-like aisles, the scent of old paper and ink filling the air. The soft murmur of the canal outside provided a serene backdrop to their exploration. Michael's fingers traced the spines of the books absentmindedly, his mind preoccupied with the conversation he knew he needed to have.

"Marco," Michael began, his voice tinged with nervous determination, "I've been thinking a lot about us, and there's something I want to talk to you about."

Marco turned to face him, concern etching his features. "Of course. What is it?"

Michael took a deep breath, gathering his thoughts.

"I'm really enjoying our time together, and the slow build-up of our connection has been intense and exciting. But I have to admit, it's driving me a little crazy. I find myself second-guessing whether you're actually attracted to me or if you just see me as a friend."

The tension between them grew palpable as Marco listened intently. He reached out and gently squeezed Michael's hand, his touch warm and reassuring. "Michael, I appreciate your honesty. I want you to know that I am genuinely attracted to you, and I care for you deeply. But..."

Michael's heart sank, sensing the possibility of disappointment. Marco continued, his voice soft yet sincere, "I understand that my pace might not be what you're used to, and I apologize if that has caused you any confusion or frustration."

Relief washed over Michael, and he smiled, his tension easing. "Thank you."

Marco returned the smile, his eyes filled with warmth. "You're welcome. I've always believed that taking things slow can create a stronger, more meaningful bond. But I also understand that everyone's needs and desires are different."

Finding strength in his inner voice, Michael pressed on. "Marco, I understand and appreciate your perspective on taking things slow. But I also want to remind you that I don't live here, and I have to return to the US next week. We met on a hookup app, and while I'm thrilled that our connection has grown into something more meaningful, I don't want to leave Venice with any regrets."

Marco nodded, his expression thoughtful. "I hear you."

Michael's smile widened, feeling a sense of mutual understanding. "I'm glad you understand. So, if we're going to fool around, let's get this show on the road. Whaddya say?"

A sly smile spread across Marco's face as he took a moment, his eyes lighting up with a mischievous glint. He leaned in closer, the space between them narrowing until Michael could feel the warmth of Marco's breath on his face, carrying with it the faintest hint of soap and the undeniable heat of his body. It was a moment of raw closeness, where the boundaries blurred, and Michael found himself lost in Marco's captivating gaze.

"I think you're ready," Marco whispered, his voice low and intimate.

Michael felt a mixture of confusion and curiosity, tempted to roll his eyes but instead finding himself drawn deeper into the moment. "Ready for what, exactly?" he asked, his voice barely more than a whisper.

Marco's smile grew, his eyes never leaving Michael's. "Ready for this," he said softly, closing the remaining distance between them and capturing Michael's lips in a kiss that was both tender and electrifying. The world around them seemed to fade away, leaving only the two of them and the unspoken promises of what was to come.

Chapter 35

In a flurry of excitement, Marco and Michael, hand in hand, raced through the weathered doors of an old *palazzo*. Their heartbeats pounded in rhythm with the urgency of their desire, each step echoing their shared anticipation. The ancient building stood as a testament to centuries past, its grandeur weathered yet still palpable.

They bounded up the marble steps, the echoes of their footsteps blending with the distant whispers of the past. The staircase spiraled upward, each turn bringing them closer to the top floor where Marco's apartment awaited. The ornate railings, cool and smooth under their hands, seemed to guide them on their journey.

Crossing the threshold beneath the flickering glow of a vintage glass chandelier, Michael felt the last vestiges of restraint crumble within him. The unquenchable flame of desire threatened to consume him as he pulled Marco close. Their lips met in a searing kiss, tongues twisting and exploring with fervent abandon. The taste of Marco's lips was intoxicating, a blend of passion and longing that left Michael dizzy.

Fumbling with eagerness, Michael's fingers found the top button of Marco's shirt. He clumsily worked to release it from its confines, but the urgency of their desire made patience impossible. In a surge of passion, he tore open Marco's shirt, the buttons flying across the room like a scattering of stars, clinking softly as they landed on the polished wooden floor.

But just as their fervor reached its peak, Marco pulled back, leaving Michael panting, hungry, and disoriented. The sudden pause was jarring, the silence between them filled with unspoken questions.

"Wait," Marco said firmly. The word hung in the air, laden with uncertainty. Michael's eyes, wide with a mixture of confusion and unfulfilled desire, searched Marco's face for an explanation, for a reason behind the sudden pause in their passionate dance.

Marco, his chest heaving, paused for a moment, eyes closed as he took several deep, grounding breaths. Michael waited, his anticipation simmering, but Marco seemed intent on deliberately slowing their pace. With measured movements, Marco patted down his hair, tucking disheveled strands behind his ears, as if reclaiming a sense of control over the unfolding scene.

Slowly, Marco's eyes met Michael's once again. He leaned closer, his voice soft and low, each word a silken thread weaving a spell around them. "Now, we'll have sex," Marco said, his tone filled with promise. "But what I'd like you to do is think about each of the five senses while we are. One sense at a time."

The seductive melody of his Italian accent lingered in the air, heightening the allure of his proposal. Michael's confusion was replaced by a sense of intrigue. Marco's approach was different, intentional, and it piqued Michael's curiosity.

Marco continued, his voice a gentle invitation for Michael to delve into the depths of his senses. "What do you hear?" he asked, leaning in to whisper into Michael's ear. The proximity sent shivers down Michael's spine, the warmth of Marco's breath a tantalizing prelude to what was to come.

Marco sensed Michael's fluttering anticipation, his nervous excitement. With a dash to the lights, he took control of the atmosphere. "This will help you," Marco said softly, and with that, he extinguished the light, plunging the room into an all-consuming darkness.

In the pitch black, every sound was amplified. Michael focused on the rustling of their clothes, the soft creak of the floorboards, the distant hum of the city outside, and the steady rhythm of Marco's breathing. Each noise seemed to wrap around them, creating an intimate symphony that heightened every sensation.

The room remained cloaked in darkness, a thick veil that rendered their world into a tapestry of sounds and sensations. Marco's voice, an intimate murmur within the void, guided Michael through the experience.

"Allow your ears to swim into my body," Marco whispered, his breath warm against Michael's ear.

In the inky blackness, Michael's senses heightened. He felt the warmth of Marco's breath on his ear and neck, the sensation sending shivers down his spine. The sound of Marco's breathing was unmistakable, and then, as if to further underscore the point, Marco blew gently into Michael's ear. The soft exhalation elicited a moan from Michael, his heart pounding in exhilaration.

"What else do you hear?" Marco asked, his voice a whisper in the dark.

Michael focused on the sounds around him, his own breaths echoing in his ears. "I hear my voice," he said, his tone trembling with excitement. "The sounds of my breath and yours."

They continued their auditory dance, Marco's voice guiding them through a symphony of sounds. In the secret blackness, they heard the rustle of fabric, the distant echoes of footsteps on the *palazzo's* stairwell, the whispers of the ancient building itself, and the tender sighs of each other's breath.

"I'm so hard... throbbing," Michael admitted, his voice thick with desire.

The darkness served as both a shroud and an invitation. Marco continued to guide Michael through the depths of connection and desire using only the power of sound. "What do you hear when I do this?" Marco asked, his tone velvet and inviting.

The sound of fabric being removed, perhaps Michael's pants, followed by the firm grip against hard skin, filled the air. Michael gasped at the touch. "Yes, that's right," Marco said, his voice on fire with passion. "I hear you, too, surprised and wanting. I like the way you sound when I touch you. Focus on hearing, despite what I'm doing down here. Listen to the sounds outside. Hear the seagulls?"

As if on cue, the distant cries of seagulls drifted through the darkness, their voices melding with the whispered echoes of the city. Just then, the cathedral bells began to ring at the top of the hour, their sonorous peals filling the air.

"*Si*, the bells," Marco breathed, his voice a shimmering thread weaving through the symphony of sounds.

Michael moaned, his senses overwhelmed by the auditory landscape and the physical sensations.

"Listen to the sounds my tongue makes as it glides

along the length of your cock," Marco whispered, his voice dripping with desire.

The sounds of wetness and moistness filled the room, accompanied by Michael's groans of pleasure. "Oh my god. Oh my god," Michael gasped, his voice strained with ecstasy.

Marco's voice, gentle and rhythmic, continued to weave a tapestry of sound as he spoke to Michael in the enveloping darkness. "That's right," he murmured. "Allow yourself to be swept away by the cosmic orchestra that plays the soundtrack of the universe. As you listen, begin to let go of your limitations, your fears, and your past experiences. Open your mind to the possibility of a new way of thinking, a fresh perspective that transcends the boundaries of your previous understanding."

Michael's mind swirled with Marco's words, the intensity of the experience heightening with each passing moment.

"This experience about the human condition is the greatest you will ever witness – a living, breathing testament to the power of self-discovery," Marco continued. "Embrace the sounds and vibrations that echo within you. Unlock the hidden chambers of your mind. Now, whenever you're ready, get ready to step into a world of boundless possibilities, as you embrace this newfound awareness, prepare to embark on a journey of transformation that will forever change the course of your life."

Marco's voice grew stronger, more insistent. "Are you ready?" he asked.

"Yes," Michael responded, his voice filled with anticipation.

And then, with a suddenness that jolted Michael's

senses, Marco turned on the light. The room was flooded with brightness, illuminating their intertwined bodies and the raw intimacy they shared. The transition from darkness to light was almost overwhelming, but Michael felt a sense of clarity and connection that transcended the physical.

Marco's hand released the switch, and he turned back to Michael, a gentle smile on his lips.

"Now, take in everything that you see. The colors of the ceiling, that painting over there. Every bit of light from the Murano glass chandelier. Take it all in."

As he spoke, the room's sound dissolved into an enveloping silence, leaving only the visual richness of their surroundings. The colors of the ceiling were a soft, creamy white with intricate frescoes painted in pastel shades. A vibrant painting hung on the far wall, depicting a lively Venetian street scene, its bright hues almost pulsating in the stillness. The Murano glass chandelier above them glittered like a constellation, its myriad colors refracting light into a dazzling display.

Marco stepped back, beginning to remove his clothing with deliberate, slow movements. Each article of clothing fell away, revealing the contours of his sinewy, muscular body, every shadow cast by his movements adding depth to his form. His skin was adorned with a clean layer of fur that gleamed under the chandelier's light.

Michael's eyes widened in wonder, taking in the sight before him. Marco's arms were long ropes of muscle, his chest defined with a deep divide between his big, square pecs, all coated in light brown fur. His torso formed a classic V-shape, his belly ribbed with muscle, a thick line of hair leading down to his groin.

Marco's mouth moved as he spoke, but no sound

emerged. He touched himself, running his fingers lightly over his right nipple, then his left. Michael's mouth watered as Marco took his hand and glided it through the treasure trail of hair running down the center of his chest and defined stomach. Marco was a vision of strength and sensuality.

Marco's lips moved next to Michael's ear, their closeness exuding intimacy and connection. The lighting cast warm, inviting shadows on their skin, every movement a silent symphony of desire.

Marco removed the remaining clothing from Michael's body, leaving him naked. The two men stood facing each other, their eyes locked in an unspoken dialogue. Marco gently guided Michael backward onto the bed and knelt down.

In total silence, Michael's face contorted with pleasure, his whimpers and moans visible but unheard. His eyes roved the room, absorbing every detail: the frescoed ceiling, Marco's head moving rhythmically, the mirror reflecting their bodies in profile, the window letting in the soft evening light, the chandelier twinkling like stars, and the artwork adding color to the scene.

Extreme close-ups captured Michael's eyes as he took everything in, fully immersed in the visual experience.

Marco stood and moved closer, climbing onto Michael's body, placing his hand firmly on Michael's chest. As he spoke, his voice gradually became audible, breaking the silence.

"Now, I invite you to experience everything you can feel," Marco whispered.

A rising blast of subsonic bass filled the room, its vibrations palpable, moving through them and inviting the viewer to become a participant in their intimate connection.

Marco's lips moved close to Michael's ear as his hands explored Michael's body. Michael's face was a canvas of emotions, his eyes fluttering closed in ecstasy. Marco's hands traced the contours of Michael's muscles, each touch sending ripples of sensation through him. Shadows and light danced across their bodies, highlighting the raw beauty of their union.

Marco's voice, now fully audible, guided Michael through the experience, encouraging him to surrender to every sensation. The deep, resonant bass vibrated through them, heightening every touch, every whisper, every breath.

"Feel my touch, Michael," Marco murmured, his voice a low, hypnotic cadence. "Feel the warmth of my skin against yours, the beat of my heart, the depth of our connection."

Michael's senses were overwhelmed, each touch magnified by the resonance of the bass, the sensation of Marco's hands exploring every inch of his body, the warmth of his breath, the softness of his lips. The world outside ceased to exist as they became lost in the rhythm of their shared passion, the silence and sound blending into a symphony of physical and emotional intimacy.

In that moment, time seemed to stand still, and Michael surrendered completely to the experience, his body and soul intertwined with Marco's, the boundaries between them dissolving into a seamless dance of love and desire.

Marco's voice was a velvety whisper in the darkness. "Let your awareness expand. Feel the texture of my skin beneath your fingertips, the hardness of my cock as it brushes against your skin, the warmth and heat as it teases your hole."

As Marco lifted Michael's legs, they instinctively wrapped around Marco's waist. He bent down, kissing Michael deeply, his lips a tantalizing promise. Michael groaned with desire, his body a live wire of sensation. Marco's breath mingled with his, their mouths moving in a fervent dance.

"Allow yourself to connect with the energy that courses through your body," Marco murmured against Michael's lips. "Feel it resonating with the energy that exists within and all around us. Feel your body welcoming me, letting me inside you. Feel me sliding into you."

Michael whimpered and moaned as Marco began to move, his thrusts slow and deliberate. Each motion was a carefully crafted symphony of pleasure and connection.

"Embrace not only the sensations of contact," Marco continued, his voice a low, hypnotic hum, "but also the emotions that flow from within—the love and vulnerability, the joy and passion. Let your heart open up to the universe as we dive into the depths of our being, discovering the infinite well of feelings that make us who we are."

Michael's face contorted with pleasure, his moans and whimpers filling the room. "Oh my god," he breathed, his voice trembling with intensity.

Marco's movements were deliberate and unhurried. "Feel it, savor it, appreciate it. There's no rush. Enjoy each moment, each sensation." He leaned over to kiss Michael, their lips meeting in a tender embrace. "Now, shift your focus to everything you taste."

Marco's tongue traced the outline of Michael's lips,

tasting him, teasing him. Michael responded eagerly, their tongues dancing together, exploring each other. "Salty," Michael murmured, savoring the taste.

Marco continued to move their bodies together slowly, lifting his arm to the headboard to brace himself, placing his armpit directly above Michael's face. Michael inhaled deeply, the scent intoxicating.

"Tell me," Marco urged, his voice a gentle command.

Michael closed his eyes, pushing his face into Marco's armpit. "You're spicy, fresh. I don't know how, but you smell like a campfire, too. Like the outdoors, like we're in the woods."

Marco smiled, his voice a soft caress. "Take your time. We're not rushing toward anything. We're here, together. Go ahead, take me in."

Michael's senses were heightened, every touch, every taste, every scent amplified in the intimacy of the moment. He breathed deeply, letting the sensations wash over him, feeling Marco's presence in every fiber of his being. The connection between them was profound, a tapestry of sensory experiences woven together in the silence of the room.

Michael was stunned by the feelings welling up inside him. His body responded with involuntary shudders, muscle spasms, and waves of pure sexual adrenaline. All his senses were awake and alive, crackling with sensation. For the first time in his life, he felt fully present, as if what they were doing was the only thing in the world, the only thing happening, the only thing that mattered.

Every touch, every breath, every whisper from Marco became a revelation. With each discovery, Michael's mind marveled at the intensity of the experience. "Whoa, what is this!? What a marvel this is," he thought, his mind barely able to comprehend the depth of pleasure and connection he was feeling.

The sound around them built to a crescendo, a symphony of their shared ecstasy, before exploding like a supernova bursting into the universe as they reached orgasm. The moment of rapture was intense, the music and cacophony of effects and design smashing out to reveal only Michael's moans. His whole body shook with the aftershocks of their climax.

His head fell back against the bed, chest heaving as he tried to capture his breath and return to the planet. Marco glided up against him, sweaty and slick, their arms entwining. They lay still, locked in the embrace, as Michael's breathing gradually returned to normal. The room, now filled with the quiet aftermath of their passion, felt like a sanctuary. The world outside ceased to exist, leaving only the profound connection between them.

Chapter 36

Bathed in moonlight, Michael stood naked before the floor-to-ceiling windows, his body illuminated by the silvery glow. The rich navy of the night sky stretched out beyond the glass, a serene backdrop to the tranquility of the moment. He felt a profound sense of peace, a stark contrast to the turmoil that had once plagued him.

"I can still taste you on my tongue," Michael said, his voice soft and reflective.

Marco, lounging naked on the bed, took a slow drag from his cigarette. The smoke curled lazily around him, adding an air of mystery to his already captivating presence. "The taste of memory... *Vorresti del vino?*" he asked, his Italian accent wrapping around the words like a lover's caress.

Michael nodded, his curiosity piqued by the promise of wine. As Marco rose from the bed, Michael followed him into the kitchen, his eyes drawn to the elegant lines of Marco's body, the way the moonlight caressed his skin.

Marco opened a bottle of wine with practiced ease, the pop of the cork echoing softly in the spacious kitchen. Michael wandered around the enormous *palazzo*, his senses heightened by the night's events. He explored the rooms and terraces, each one offering a new discovery.

The artwork lining the walls was incredible, each piece telling a story of its own. One painting, in particular, caught his eye—could it be an actual Picasso? The thought intrigued him, adding another layer of enchantment to the night.

Marco found him standing before the painting, lost in thought. He approached silently, handing Michael a glass of wine. "*Saluti*," Marco said, his voice a gentle interruption to Michael's reverie.

"*Saluti*," Michael replied, their eyes locking as they raised their glasses in a toast. The clink of the crystal was the only sound in the room, a delicate punctuation to the moment.

They shared a long and tender kiss, the taste of wine mingling with the lingering flavors of their passion. The kiss deepened, a silent communication of the connection they had forged. Michael felt a surge of emotion, a mix of gratitude and desire that left him breathless.

The night seemed to stretch on forever, a timeless expanse filled with the promise of new beginnings. Marco's touch was a balm to Michael's soul, each caress a reminder of the beauty that could be found in vulnerability and trust.

As they stood there, bathed in moonlight and wrapped in each other's arms, the world outside ceased to matter. All that existed was the here and now, the intoxicating blend of love, desire, and the exquisite magic of Venice.

Chapter 37

Marco and Michael walked side by side through the narrow, winding streets of Venice. The cobblestone beneath their feet created a rhythmic clack, a soft melody accompanying their steps. The air was crisp, each exhaled breath visible as a puff of steam, mingling and dissipating in the cool night air. Michael licked his lips, savoring the lingering taste of Marco's sweetness. The memory of their shared intimacy was fresh, making his senses more acute, the world around him more vibrant.

The city was alive with a quiet magic. The moonlight bathed the ancient buildings in a silvery glow, casting long, soft shadows that danced with the flicker of gas lamps. *Gondolas* swayed gently in the canals, their reflections rippling across the water. The scent of the sea mixed with the aroma of nearby trattorias, creating a heady blend that was distinctly Venetian.

As they neared the entrance of Michael's hotel, a grand building with ivy-clad walls and ornate balconies, Marco turned to him. His eyes held a warm, yet matter-of-fact expression.

"Good job. I'll see you tomorrow. Meet me at my place," Marco said, his voice steady and calm.

"Of course..." Michael replied, his voice tinged with a mix of anticipation and longing.

Marco smiled, a brief but genuine expression that warmed Michael's heart. Without a kiss, hug, or handshake, Marco turned and walked away, the sound of his shoes on the cobblestone echoing in the quiet street. Michael watched until Marco's figure disappeared into the labyrinth of Venice, the night swallowing him up.

Inside the hotel, Michael made his way to his room, the grandeur of the lobby with its marble floors and opulent chandeliers barely registering in his mind. His thoughts were a whirlwind of pleasure and anticipation, each memory of the evening replaying in vivid detail.

He collapsed onto the bed, the soft Italian linens caressing his skin. The sensation was almost sensual, the fine fabric cool against his legs. He kicked off his shoes and stretched out, feeling the stability of the hotel bed beneath him. The firmness of the pillows cradled his head, providing a comfort that felt almost luxurious.

His senses were on overdrive. The taste of Marco still lingered on his lips, the scent of his cologne clinging faintly to his clothes. The sound of their laughter, their whispered words, echoed in his mind. He could still feel the warmth of Marco's touch, the gentle pressure of his hands, the brush of his lips.

Michael's mind drifted, each sensation blending into the next. He felt the coolness of the room, the faint hum of the city outside, the distant sound of water lapping against the canal walls. His heart beat steadily, a rhythmic reminder of the life pulsing through his veins, the emotions surging through his soul.

He closed his eyes, letting the memories wash over him, each one a wave of pleasure and contentment. Marco's face appeared in his mind's eye, his smile, his eyes, the way he moved, the sound of his voice. Michael felt a deep sense of connection, a bond that transcended the physical, touching something deeper within him.

As sleep began to claim him, Michael's last conscious thought was of Marco, and the promise of tomorrow. The anticipation of seeing him again, of exploring their connection further, filled him with a warmth that was almost tangible. He drifted off with a smile on his lips, his body relaxed and his heart full.

The night outside continued its quiet dance, the city of Venice embracing its secrets and stories. And in his room, Michael slept, his dreams filled with the promise of love, the magic of Venice, and the sweet, lingering taste of Marco.

Chapter 38

Breakfast with Liza was a calming ritual amidst the bustling life of Venice. The small café where they sat was filled with the aroma of freshly brewed coffee and the sweet scent of pastries. The morning sun cast a warm glow on the cobblestone streets, making the city look even more enchanting.

Michael leaned back in his chair, a soft smile playing on his lips as he recounted the previous night's events. The café was alive with the gentle clinking of espresso cups on saucers and the murmur of conversation, but for Michael, the world had narrowed down to this intimate exchange with Liza.

"It was intense," Michael began, his eyes reflecting a mix of wonder and apprehension. "I suddenly felt self-conscious, or somehow exposed. It was like he was seeing me... or looking right through me. I felt utterly transparent, like he could see into my heart, what I felt, and what I thought. It was wonderful and nerve-racking."

Liza raised an eyebrow, her curiosity piqued. "Wow, that does sound intense. How did it feel?" she asked, leaning in slightly, her attention fully on Michael.

Michael took a sip of his coffee, letting the rich flavor soothe his nerves. "I was desperate for it," he admitted. "My ex never accepted or showed any interest in me.

With Bernie, it had been all business, cold and surface, nothing sensual or kind. And I felt like Marco could see that. See me. I started wondering, is the cliché about Europeans taking lovers and being great lovers true? Or am I living in a dream?"

Liza listened intently, her eyes softening with empathy. "And what did you think?" she prompted, her voice gentle and encouraging.

Michael exhaled, feeling the weight of his realizations. "It suddenly occurred to me that the entire time I was with my ex, I had externalized my senses... all of them. My internal feelings and experiences had taken the back burner. I had been more dedicated to what the other person had, felt, and sensed. I had neglected my inner sense of self for more than a decade."

Liza nodded, her expression thoughtful. "So what changed?" she asked, her curiosity evident.

Michael's eyes sparkled with a newfound energy as he continued. "Last night woke me up. My spirit and soul returned to my body. It was more than just sex. It was a new understanding and the awareness of being alive. My senses flooded back into me with a spectacular roar."

He took a bite of his croissant, savoring the buttery, flaky texture. The simple act of eating felt like a celebration of life. "You know what? It felt like it was the first time I'd had sex in my life. Everything was so new and profound. Plus, there was something else I noticed."

Liza's curiosity deepened. "What?" she asked, leaning closer.

Michael's voice lowered conspiratorially. "There was enough REAL art on the walls to suggest Marco is more than a plain ole calligraphy teacher."

Liza's eyes widened with intrigue. "Really? What kind

of art?" she asked, her tone a mix of excitement and skepticism.

Michael took another bite, his mind replaying the images of Marco's *palazzo*. "There were pieces that looked like they belonged in a museum. One even looked like a Picasso. But could it be an actual Picasso? Maybe. The whole place was filled with incredible artwork. It made me realize that there's so much more to Marco than meets the eye."

Liza leaned back, processing Michael's words. "Wow, that's amazing. It sounds like you're not just falling for him, but also discovering so many new things about yourself and the world around you."

Michael nodded, his heart swelling with gratitude for the journey he was on. "Exactly. It's like I'm finally waking up to life, feeling every moment, and appreciating the beauty in everything. And Marco... he's a big part of that."

They sat in companionable silence for a moment, savoring their breakfast and the warmth of the morning sun. The café around them buzzed with life, but within their little bubble, it was a moment of pure connection and understanding.

As Michael finished his coffee, he felt a sense of peace and excitement for the future. He knew that whatever happened, he was on a path of self-discovery and growth, and he was ready to embrace it fully.

Chapter 39

In the dimly lit hotel room, Michael sat at the small desk facing his laptop. The soft glow from the screen cast gentle shadows across his face, illuminating his thoughtful expression. Outside, the sounds of Venice filtered through the window – the distant hum of boats on the canal, the occasional laughter of passersby, and the ever-present symphony of the city's life.

Dr. Gika's face appeared on the screen, her warm smile radiating a comforting energy even through the digital barrier. Michael adjusted his position, feeling a sense of anticipation mixed with relief. This was a space where he could explore his feelings openly.

"Michael, it sounds like what you experienced last night is what I call conscious sex," Dr. Gika began, her tone gentle yet profound. "Conscious sex is a powerful and transformative approach to intimacy. It goes beyond just physical connection."

Michael leaned forward, his interest piqued. "Yes, that sounds exactly right," he responded, his voice filled with a mix of curiosity and understanding.

Dr. Gika continued, her eyes reflecting a depth of knowledge and empathy. "When we engage in conscious sex, we are fully present in the moment, connecting our minds, bodies, and spirits with our partner. This connection transcends the barriers of ego, allowing us to experience a profound sense of unity and oneness. It's about truly seeing and honoring the other person, as well as ourselves."

Michael nodded, the words resonating deeply with him. "I feel like all the sex I've had in the past was totally unconscious. With Marco, it felt like our souls were connected."

"That's wonderful, Michael," Dr. Gika said, her smile broadening. "As you continue to explore consciousness in all forms, you'll find that it nurtures emotional and spiritual growth, deepens intimacy, and promotes overall well-being. This form of lovemaking encourages true vulnerability, trust, and communication between partners, allowing you to form a powerful bond that transcends the physical realm."

Michael listened intently, absorbing each word like a sponge. The room seemed to fade away as he focused on Dr. Gika's voice, her wisdom providing clarity and direction. He felt a sense of liberation, as if the walls of his own limitations were beginning to crumble.

"Remember to stay open, curious, and present as you continue to explore," Dr. Gika advised, her tone soothing. "Embrace the journey, and you'll find that it has the power to transform not only your relationship with the world around you but also your relationship with yourself."

Michael sat back, a sense of peace washing over him. The soft hum of the laptop fan and the distant sounds of Venice created a tranquil backdrop to his thoughts. He felt a renewed sense of purpose and a deeper connection to himself and the experiences he was having.

"Thank you, Dr. Gika," he said sincerely. "Your guidance means so much to me. I feel like I'm finally understanding what it means to truly connect with someone."

Dr. Gika's eyes shone with pride and encouragement. "You're doing wonderfully, Michael. Keep embracing this journey of self-discovery and connection. It's a beautiful path you're on."

With the session drawing to a close, Michael felt a profound sense of gratitude. He knew that this was just the beginning of a deeper, more conscious exploration of himself and his relationships. As he closed his laptop, the room felt lighter, filled with the promise of new beginnings and the joy of genuine connection.

The night outside was calm, the moon casting a silvery light over the canals. Michael stood by the window, gazing out at the serene beauty of Venice. He felt a deep sense of contentment, knowing that he was on a path of true self-discovery and meaningful connection. The journey ahead was unknown, but for the first time in a long while, he felt ready to embrace it with an open heart and mind.

Chapter 40

Michael walked towards Marco's *palazzo* with a new sense of awareness, the world around him bursting with vivid details. The cobblestone streets, the scent of the canal, the sounds of life in Venice all seemed to pulsate with a rhythm that matched his own heartbeat. He felt alive, more present than ever before.

Entering Marco's *palazzo*, a surge of desire coursed through Michael. The grand entrance, with its elegant decor and historic charm, barely registered in his mind. His focus was solely on Marco, who stood waiting, a knowing smile playing on his lips.

"Marco!" Michael called, his voice thick with longing.

Without hesitation, he wrapped his arms around Marco, pulling him into a passionate embrace. The heat between them was palpable, their breaths mingling as they pressed close. But Marco, ever the guide in their sensual journey, placed a finger on Michael's lips, silencing him with a gentle but firm touch. The intimacy of the gesture heightened the tension, making the moment even more electrifying.

"Now," Marco whispered, his voice a soft command, "Today, what I'd like you to do is think about what you're doing and how you're doing it. And how your actions might affect MY senses."

He took Michael's hand, guiding it along his face and down his body. The tactile connection was intense, every touch sending shivers through both men. Michael began to remove Marco's clothes, the fabric sliding away to reveal the sculpted lines of his physique.

"You can imagine," Marco continued, "but you won't know for sure. Explore these things one by one. Find out. Investigate."

Naked and entwined on the bed, their bodies bathed in the golden light of the afternoon sun, Michael traced every inch of Marco's body with his tongue. He explored the planes and curves, the smoothness of skin over muscle, the taste and texture unique to Marco. Each lick, each caress, elicited whimpers and moans from Marco, sounds that fueled Michael's desire.

Michael flipped Marco onto his stomach, his hands gliding down to his ass. He worshipped Marco's body with his tongue, his hands sliding over the firm, muscular expanse. The sunlight illuminated their bodies, casting a halo around their intimate dance.

"So beautiful," Michael murmured, his voice filled with reverence.

He moved up Marco's back, tenderly licking his way along the spine, his body grinding against Marco's in a slow, deliberate rhythm. Marco turned his head, their lips meeting in a fervent kiss, the need in Marco's eyes mirroring Michael's own.

"I want to feel you inside me," Marco breathed, his voice husky with need. "I want you to fill me... completely."

They rolled together, kissing wildly, hands exploring, bodies pressing close. The air was thick with the scent of their arousal, the sound of their breathing and the soft creak of the bed adding to the symphony of their lovemaking.

"Please," Marco pleaded, his voice a desperate whisper.

"You want me to cum inside you?" Michael asked, his voice trembling with anticipation.

Marco responded in Italian, the words flowing like a sensual melody, *"Dammi tutto, ho bisogno di te."*

The intensity of their connection reached a crescendo. Michael pounded into Marco, their bodies moving in perfect harmony. His hands gripped Marco's hips, pulling him closer, deeper. Marco's face was electric, gasping for more, eyes alight with ecstasy.

Sweat dripped from Michael's face as he reached the peak of his pleasure, his body shuddering with the force of his orgasm. Marco's smile mirrored his own, a radiant expression of pure bliss as he felt Michael's release inside him.

They collapsed together, their bodies entwined, the room filled with the afterglow of their passion. The sunlight continued to bathe them, a silent witness to their intimate connection. In that moment, they were completely, utterly in tune with each other, their senses and souls intertwined in perfect harmony.

Chapter 41

In the soft, post-coital glow, Marco and Michael lay intertwined, their bodies still warm and slick from their shared passion. The room was bathed in a gentle twilight, the fading sunlight casting a golden hue over their naked forms. Marco, his breath steady and calm, placed a tender kiss on Michael's lips, savoring the intimate connection that lingered between them.

"How many colors do you see in my eyes?" Marco asked, his voice a soft murmur as he looked deeply into Michael's eyes.

Michael, feeling a profound sense of closeness, took his time, his gaze exploring the depths of Marco's eyes. He saw flecks of color dancing in the light, a kaleidoscope of hues that reflected the complexity of their connection.

"Green... Gold, yellow, orange. Green," Michael answered, his voice filled with wonder.

Marco smiled, a boyish grin that made Michael's heart flutter. "You said green already," Marco teased gently, his eyes sparkling with affection.

Michael chuckled, his fingers tracing the contours of Marco's face. "Being present and consciously aware of everything I was doing... it was like stepping into a world of magic," he said thoughtfully. "It wasn't just about me or my desires; it was about us, together, as two people fully engaged in the moment. And the more I focused on you, the more incredible the experience became for me in return."

Marco kissed his cheek, a tender gesture that spoke volumes. He then hopped out of bed with a graceful ease, leaving Michael to linger in the afterglow of their intimate encounter. The warmth of the moment stayed with Michael, wrapping around him like a comforting embrace.

From across the room, Marco's voice carried over, filled with a quiet certainty. "Very good... We'll meet again tomorrow."

Michael lay back, his thoughts drifting on the tide of their shared experience. The room, now dimmed by the approaching night, felt like a sanctuary, a place where he had discovered a new depth of connection and understanding. As he closed his eyes, the memory of Marco's touch, his voice, and the myriad colors in his eyes remained vivid, a promise of more moments to come.

Chapter 42

As Michael and Liza strolled along the Grand Canal, the shimmering reflections of the water danced in their eyes. *Gondolas* glided gracefully by, carrying loving couples who whispered sweet nothings to each other. The air was filled with the scent of the canal, a blend of history and romance, as locals went about their day, adding to the vibrant tapestry of Venice.

Michael, lost in thought, finally broke the silence. "It was unlike anything I've ever felt before," he said, his voice filled with wonder. "We shared a connection that was so much deeper... It was... transformative."

Liza, always engaged and curious, prompted him to continue. "Do tell."

Michael's eyes sparkled as he spoke. "It was as if time stopped, and we were in our own little world, just the two of us. It was a profound experience that went beyond pleasure. It was about exploring his existence, his soul, and being in tune with him."

"That sounds amazing," Liza said, genuinely happy for her friend.

"Yeah, it really is," Michael agreed, a smile spreading across his face. "I feel like a different person now, more in touch with my emotions, my desires, and my true self.

I feel... reborn. Like I've discovered a part of myself that I didn't even know existed. It's an incredible feeling."

Liza's smile was warm and supportive. "I'm so happy for you, Michael. You truly deserve this. Just remember to hold onto this feeling and let it guide you when you're back home."

"I don't think it's possible for me to forget," Michael replied, his voice filled with conviction.

Liza teased him playfully. "I'd say Marco has taught you a thing or two about being a good lover – and so much more."

Michael's expression turned sincere. "I'm really going to miss you, Liza. I can't believe you're leaving tomorrow. I'm honestly feeling a bit sad about it."

Liza's concern was evident. "I know, but I'm sure you'll be okay. Just think of all the amazing experiences you're having here, and how much you're growing as a person. You're strong and capable, and I have no doubt you'll be fine on your own."

Michael felt a deep appreciation for his friend's support. "Your support means the world to me."

"When are you coming home?" Liza asked, her tone lighter.

"Monday," Michael replied.

Liza grinned. "I'll be eagerly awaiting all the juicy details of whatever happens next."

Later, as they walked through the halls of the Peggy Guggenheim Collection, Michael felt a sense of wonder and awe with each step. The grandeur of the museum, housed within the *Palazzo Venier dei Leoni*, created a serene and inspiring atmosphere, cradling the treasures of modern art that adorned its walls.

Michael wandered through the luminous rooms and

corridors, the diverse array of artwork enchanting and captivating him. Drawn to the works of Jackson Pollock, Salvador Dalí, and Pablo Picasso, he felt his spirit soaring, his connection with the artistic visionaries deepening with each masterpiece.

But it was one painting, in particular, that stopped Michael in his tracks. The canvas, awash with a mélange of vibrant colors and mesmerizing shapes, seemed to beckon him, calling out to his very soul. As he stood before the painting, Michael felt an almost tangible connection, a profound resonance that transcended the boundaries of time and space.

The artwork appeared to be a portal into a world of emotion, a vivid landscape of the human experience, as if the artist had managed to distill a lifetime of passion, joy, and sorrow into a single, breathtaking composition. Michael, captivated by the painting's depth and intensity, felt a sudden, overwhelming sense of kinship with the artist and their journey.

This profound connection to the painting left an indelible mark on Michael's heart, a testament to the enduring power of art and its ability to inspire, provoke, and transform our perception of the world. As he stood there, absorbing every detail of the masterpiece, he felt a renewed sense of purpose and a deeper understanding of his own journey. The city of Venice, with its rich history and timeless beauty, had opened his eyes to new possibilities and the boundless potential of the human spirit.

Chapter 43

The sun rose over the quiet canals of Venice, casting a golden glow on the water's surface, illuminating the historic city with a warm, gentle light. The streets were still, and the only sounds were the faint ripples of water against the boats and the soft murmurs of morning life beginning anew.

As Liza stepped onto the speedboat, Michael was there to help her with her suitcase, carefully lifting it onto the watertaxi. The cool morning air was filled with a sense of farewell and new beginnings.

"See you when you're home!" Liza called out, her voice filled with both excitement and a touch of sadness at leaving.

"*Buon viaggio!*" Michael replied, his words sincere and warm.

The watertaxi engine started with a low rumble, and the boat slowly began to move down the canal. As it pulled away from the dock, Liza waved goodbye to Michael, her hand cutting through the morning air with grace. Michael raised his own hand in farewell, his smile unwavering as he watched his friend disappear into the distance.

Standing at the dock, Michael lingered for a moment,

taking in the beauty of the scene before him. The golden light danced on the water, creating a shimmering tapestry of reflections. He felt a sense of peace and clarity, grateful for the time spent with Liza and the memories they had made together in this enchanting city.

Turning away from the dock, Michael made his way through the narrow, winding streets of Venice. He wandered into a small Venetian mask shop, a hidden gem filled with intricate, spirited masks, each one a piece of art. The shelves were lined with masks of all shapes and sizes, adorned with feathers, jewels, and delicate lace. Michael gently fingered a beautifully adorned mask, its gilded edges catching the soft light, reflecting a kaleidoscope of colors.

Suddenly, he felt a chill run down his spine. A familiar, unsettling energy filled the room as Angelo entered the shop with his characteristic arrogance, a malicious grin playing on his lips. The atmosphere grew tense as Angelo's presence disrupted the serene ambiance of the shop.

Michael, feeling Angelo's presence, turned around, holding the ornate mask in his hand. Angelo made a crude sexual gesture, his smirk widening as he locked eyes with Michael.

"Quite fitting to find you here, don't you think?" Michael said, his voice calm and composed, masking the unease he felt inside.

Angelo, taken aback by Michael's composure, smirked. "What's that supposed to mean? Come suck my dick," he sneered.

Michael, maintaining his calm demeanor, raised the mask he was holding. Its mirrorlike surface caught

Angelo's incredulous gaze, reflecting his own distorted image back at him.

"Turns out, life can be one big masquerade, right?" Michael said with newfound clarity. "We all walk around in masks we've picked out, some more flashy than others. For a while there, I was just like everyone else, hiding behind my own mask, wearing my own disguise. And in that game of pretending, somehow you showed up."

Michael's tone softened as he continued, his words carrying a weight of introspection. "But I've figured out how to take off my mask, how to step out of my costume and let the world see the real me. I've learned to want more – connections that aren't just skin-deep, but ones that reach right down into the soul."

He turned serious, looking Angelo straight in the eye. Angelo squirmed under his gaze, the arrogance in his expression faltering.

"I'm very grateful to have met you," Michael said sincerely. "You gave me a wake-up call I didn't know I needed."

His voice was encouraging as he gave Angelo his parting words. "I hope that one day, you'll find it in you to throw away the mask you're wearing. And when you do, you'll see the world for what it really is – a dance floor where it's not just bodies moving, but souls interacting, connecting, and living."

As Michael placed the mask back onto the shelf, a soft smile lit up his face. He turned and walked towards the door, leaving the shop with a sense of closure and peace. Surrounded by masks, Angelo stood, stunned into silence, as Michael exited the shop and stepped back into the vibrant streets of Venice.

Chapter 44

In Marco's *palazzo*, the moonlight poured through the expansive windows, bathing the room in a silvery glow. Both men stood naked, their bodies illuminated by the soft, ethereal light. Michael stared into Marco's eyes, his face not a foot away, feeling an electric connection that transcended the physical.

Michael's voice was a whisper, filled with anticipation. "What now?"

Marco's eyes sparkled with an enigmatic intensity. "Now, I want you to combine all we've experienced and learned about each other. We will meld. There will be no barriers to where your senses end and mine begin. Only oneness. We'll combine our bodies and all our senses at once, all together. At the same time."

As if painted by the delicate brushstrokes of fate, Marco's voice was a soft melody that seemed to possess a life of its own. The very air around them shimmered with the enchanting resonance of his words, conjuring images that danced and flickered like embers on the edge of dreams.

The room transformed before Michael's eyes into a visual symphony, a kaleidoscope of shifting colors and shapes that ebbed and flowed to the rhythm of Marco's voice. The images, at once so near and yet so distant, moved in and out of focus, their edges blurring as they merged and transformed, giving birth to new visions with each passing second.

Glimmering lights of refraction and illumination played across Michael's senses, casting the world in a fantastical, almost otherworldly glow. It was as if the universe itself had opened its heart, revealing the secrets of its celestial dance in a dazzling display of cosmic artistry.

This supernova of light and sound seemed to bend the very fabric of reality. The pulsating rhythm transported Michael to a realm where the infinite beauty of the cosmos lay at their fingertips. He could feel Marco's presence, not just beside him, but within him, their essences intertwining in a dance of pure, unfiltered emotion.

As their bodies moved closer, the warmth of Marco's skin against his own sent shivers of pleasure through Michael. He could feel Marco's heartbeat, strong and steady, syncing with his own. Their breaths mingled, each inhale and exhale a testament to their shared desire and connection.

Michael's fingers traced the contours of Marco's body, feeling the firm muscles beneath the smooth skin, the light layer of fur that gleamed in the moonlight. Every touch was a spark, igniting a fire that burned brightly between them. Marco's hands roamed over Michael's back, pulling him closer, until there was no space left between them.

The sounds of their combined breaths, the gentle moans of pleasure, the soft rustle of their movements created a symphony that resonated through the room. It was a harmony of passion and tenderness, a testament to the bond they had forged.

Marco's voice, a low, seductive whisper, guided Michael further into this realm of heightened senses. "Feel the texture of my skin beneath your fingertips, the hardness of my body as it presses against yours, the warmth and heat as our bodies merge."

Michael's senses were on hyperdrive, each touch, each sensation magnified in the intimate silence. He could feel every ridge and curve of Marco's body, the way his muscles tensed and relaxed with each movement. The scent of Marco's skin, a mix of earthy musk and something uniquely him, filled his nostrils, grounding him in the present moment.

Marco's words were a gentle murmur in the darkness, a guide through the symphony of sensations. "Allow yourself to connect with the energy that courses through your body, and feel it resonating with the energy that exists within and all around us."

Michael's mind was a whirl of colors and sounds, each sense heightened to an almost unbearable degree. He could feel the energy flowing between them, a current of pure, unadulterated desire. Marco's lips found his, their kisses deep and passionate, a dance of tongues and teeth that left Michael breathless.

They moved together, their bodies entwined in a dance of pure, unrestrained passion. Michael could feel Marco inside him, filling him completely, each thrust sending waves of pleasure through his body. The rhythm of their movements was a symphony, a perfect harmony of desire and connection.

Marco's voice was a whisper against his ear, each word a caress. "Embrace not only the sensations of contact, but also the emotions that flow from within, the love and vulnerability, the joy and passion. Let your heart open up to the universe, as we dive into the depths of our being, discovering the infinite well of feelings that make us who we are."

Michael's world was reduced to the sensation of Marco's body against his, the feel of his skin, the sound of his breath, the taste of his kiss. He was lost in the moment, a willing participant in the dance of their combined senses.

As they reached the peak of their passion, the world seemed to explode in a burst of light and sound. The sensation was overwhelming, a supernova of pleasure that left Michael breathless, his body trembling with the force of his orgasm. The sound crescendoed and exploded like a supernova bursting into the universe, leaving only the sound of Michael's moans, his whole body shaking.

Marco glided up against him, sweaty and slick, their arms entwined. They lay still, locked in the embrace, as Michael's breathing returned to normal. In the afterglow of their passion, they found a sense of peace, a connection that transcended the physical, a bond forged in the fire of their shared experience.

For the first time in his life, Michael felt fully present, as if what they were doing was the only thing in the world, the only thing happening. The only thing that mattered. With each discovery: Whoa, what is this!? What a marvel this is.

Naked, Marco and Michael lay entwined, their bodies glowing in the aftermath of their ethereal experience. The room was bathed in a soft, shimmering light, casting shadows that danced across the walls like ethereal spirits. The air was filled with the gentle hum of their shared breaths, the intimacy of their connection creating an almost tangible warmth that enveloped them.

Michael's head rested on Marco's chest, Marco's strong arms wrapped protectively around him. Michael's voice, filled with wonder and awe, broke the serene silence. "At moments, our souls seemed to merge, and I couldn't tell where I ended, and you began, or the other way around. I felt a wholeness... or the oneness you mentioned. I've never experienced that before."

Marco listened intently, his hand gently caressing Michael's arm and shoulder, the touch soothing and intimate. His eyes held a depth of understanding and empathy that mirrored Michael's own.

"When I came... my legs started shaking... I felt my heart and soul fill with a brilliant white light..." Michael's voice trailed off, his eyes reflecting the profound impact of the experience.

Marco's caresses continued, each stroke a silent acknowledgment of the bond they had forged. The soft glow of the room highlighted the contours of their intertwined bodies, emphasizing the connection that went beyond the physical.

"My body became a starry explosion from a firework sending glittering sparks in all directions. Like a supernova." Michael's voice trembled slightly, the memory of the sensation still vivid. "In that moment, I understood the universe."

A tender silence filled the room, Michael's words hanging in the air like a delicate echo. The profound connection they had shared illuminated the depths of their souls, allowing them to touch the infinite expanse of the cosmos. The room seemed to hold its breath, the atmosphere charged with the intensity of their union.

Marco's voice, soft and filled with gratitude, broke the silence. *"Grazie mille."*

A tear escaped Marco's eye as he leaned down and tenderly kissed Michael's forehead, the gesture a silent promise of the depth of his feelings. Michael's heart swelled with a mixture of love and contentment, the warmth of Marco's embrace grounding him in the present moment.

The soft, shimmering light continued to dance around them, casting a gentle glow that seemed to blend their bodies and souls into one. The universe, with all its mysteries and wonders, felt closer than ever, contained within the intimate space they shared.

In that moment, nothing else mattered. The world outside faded into insignificance as they lay together, their hearts beating in perfect harmony. The connection they had forged was a testament to the power of love and vulnerability, a reminder that true intimacy went beyond the physical to touch the very essence of their being.

Michael closed his eyes, allowing the sensations and emotions to wash over him. He felt a sense of peace and fulfillment that he had never known before, a contentment that came from being truly seen and understood. The soft rhythm of Marco's heartbeat beneath his ear was a soothing lullaby, lulling him into a state of blissful relaxation.

As the night wore on, the soft light began to fade, replaced by the gentle glow of dawn creeping through the windows. Michael and Marco remained entwined, their bodies and souls still connected in a dance of love and unity. The world outside began to stir, but within the sanctuary of the room, time seemed to stand still.

In the quiet moments before the world awakened, Michael whispered, "Thank you, Marco. For everything."

Marco's embrace tightened slightly, his voice a gentle murmur. "No, thank you, Michael. For opening your heart to me."

And as the first rays of sunlight touched their faces, they knew that their journey together was just beginning, a journey filled with endless possibilities and the promise of a love that transcended the boundaries of the physical world.

Chapter 45

Michael wandered through the narrow cobblestone streets of Venice, the city now alive with a vibrant new energy. The world around him seemed to pulsate with a renewed sense of magic, as if the very fabric of reality had shifted beneath his feet. The canals glittered under the soft morning light, their waters reflecting the splendor of the ancient buildings lining their banks. *Gondolas* glided gracefully by, their *gondoliers'* songs echoing through the narrow alleyways.

As Michael turned a corner, he came upon a group of people gathered around a woman standing on a makeshift stage. The woman held a microphone and addressed the crowd in fluent English. The atmosphere buzzed with anticipation and excitement, the air charged with a sense of celebration.

Michael was drawn to the woman's voice, her words carrying an air of enchantment. He approached the gathering, curiosity etched across his face. The crowd around him was a mosaic of faces, each one reflecting the shared joy and anticipation of the moment.

The woman's voice was full of truth as she spoke. "To the work that left our audience with tears of emotion..." she began, her tone sincere and resonant. "Your extraordinary ability to envision the recovery of one's self and the acceptance of one's inclinations, regardless of social roles, is truly inspiring. You have shown us that the key to both survival and life lies in embracing who we truly are and trusting in the unknown."

The crowd listened intently, entranced by the woman's heartfelt speech. Michael stood among them, his eyes shining with the reflection of the new light he carried within. The words seemed to speak directly to his heart, resonating deeply with his own journey and experiences.

The woman continued, her voice filled with warmth and conviction. "Your message of hope has resonated deeply with us, reminding us that we can reinvent our own existence from scratch at any time, forgetting who we were for anyone before, and embracing the kindness that comes with the absence of prejudices. This is the core of any expression of love."

Michael felt a surge of emotion. The magic he felt with Marco, the profound connection and transformation, was not confined to that moment. It existed all around him, waiting to be discovered in every corner of his life.

The woman's words flowed like a soothing river. "Your use of nature, whether it be stones, trees, ocean, or animals, as a pacifying force is masterful. The way you seamlessly punctuate sound and images throughout the work is a true testament to your craft."

Michael looked down at his feet, feeling a deep sense of grounding. His mother's advice echoed in his mind, reminding him of the resilience and strength he had discovered within himself.

"Finally," the woman said, her voice softening to a poetic cadence, "the reference to the ocean as a mother's womb for every painful and outdated memory that fades away is a powerful and poetic reminder that we can let go of the past and live the life we want to live."

She paused, allowing the weight of her words to settle over the crowd. "Thank you for this beautiful and heart-wrenching work. It has touched us deeply and left an indelible mark on our souls."

The audience erupted into applause, their clapping a thunderous affirmation of the woman's sentiments. A man stepped forward to take his prize on the stage, his face a mixture of pride and humility.

As Michael stood amidst the applause, he felt a profound sense of clarity. His journey, filled with moments of revelation and connection, had only just begun. The experiences he had shared with Marco, the lessons he had learned about love and self-discovery, were now a part of his very being.

In that instant, Michael understood that life was a continuous unfolding of new beginnings. Each moment, each experience, held the potential for magic and transformation. With a heart full of hope and a spirit ready to embrace the unknown, Michael walked away from the gathering, ready to face whatever lay ahead with a newfound sense of purpose and joy.

Chapter 46

Marco and Michael sat at a tiny café table near Marco's *palazzo*. The air was filled with the soft murmur of conversations and the clinking of cups. Michael took a sip of his espresso, savoring the rich, smooth taste as it slid down his throat, leaving a warm, comforting trail.

Marco leaned forward, his eyes sparkling with a mixture of seriousness and affection. "Today, I'll teach you the most important lesson," he said, his voice a gentle murmur that seemed to blend with the ambient sounds of the café.

Michael, sensing the gravity of Marco's words, leaned in closer, his full attention on him.

"Each time you meet someone," Marco began, his tone filled with quiet conviction, "whether it be a lover, a friend, a colleague, a neighbor, or a person on the street... find something about them that you can instantly **love**."

He paused, letting his words sink in. Michael nodded, feeling the weight and wisdom of Marco's advice.

"It doesn't have to be anything big," Marco continued. "It could be their little finger, their laugh, or the way they walk. It can be anything at all so long as you can love it."

Marco's eyes twinkled as he added, "For me, it might

be that little dimple I first saw on the side of your smile."

Michael couldn't help but grin uncontrollably, a warmth spreading through him at Marco's words. The simplicity and beauty of the lesson touched him deeply.

"Whatever it is," Marco said, his voice filled with earnestness, "if you can find it and invite love and love's energy into your experience, no matter what you do with that other person... no matter what you create, what you work on, or talk about, share sexually, or engage in professionally, the process will flourish from that initial place."

He paused, his eyes locking with Michael's, the connection between them palpable. "With love, you will enhance the outcome of all that you do, no matter what."

Marco stood, reaching out his hand to Michael. Michael, his heart swelling with emotion, took Marco's hand and stood up. Marco led him across the *piazza*, the cobblestones beneath their feet echoing the steady beat of their footsteps.

They reached the grand entrance of Marco's *palazzo* and began to climb the marble stairs, each step a testament to the journey they had shared. The marble felt cool under their feet, contrasting with the warmth radiating between them.

As they ascended, Michael's thoughts drifted to the countless moments they had experienced together, each one imbued with a sense of discovery and love. The lessons he had learned from Marco had transformed him, opening his heart and mind in ways he had never imagined.

When they reached the top, they paused for a moment, taking in the view of the city below. The soft light of the setting sun bathed Venice in a golden glow, casting long shadows that danced across the rooftops and canals.

Marco turned to Michael, his expression tender and full of love. "Remember, Michael, it all begins with love," he said softly.

Michael nodded, feeling the truth of Marco's words resonate within him. He leaned in and kissed Marco gently, a kiss filled with gratitude, love, and a promise of many more moments to come.

Together, they entered the *palazzo*, their hearts intertwined, ready to face whatever the future held, with love as their guiding star.

Chapter 47

Marco and Michael approached the entrance to the hotel, their steps slowing as they neared the threshold. The air between them was thick with unspoken words and the weight of impending separation. The soft glow of the streetlights cast a warm hue over their faces, highlighting the deep connection that had formed between them.

Marco turned to Michael, his eyes filled with a mixture of tenderness and resolve. "Michael, before we part ways, I want to give you something to remember our time together," he said, his voice steady but imbued with emotion.

He reached into his pocket and retrieved a small silver coin, its surface glinting softly in the light. Etched onto the coin was the image of an acorn, detailed and intricate. Marco gently placed the coin into Michael's hand, their fingers lingering together, the warmth of their touch speaking volumes.

"This acorn symbolizes planting good seeds in life," Marco continued, his gaze never leaving Michael's. "Every moment we spend with those we love is a seed, one that can grow into something beautiful and lasting like a mighty oak. I want you to remember to cherish every moment, no matter where life takes you."

Michael looked down at the coin, feeling the weight of its significance. His voice quivered with emotion as he spoke. "Thank you, Marco. This... this means more to me than you can imagine."

Marco's eyes softened as he gazed deeply into Michael's. "No matter where our journeys take us, know that I love you, Michael, and I always will. As you move forward in life, remember to treasure every moment, every connection, every heartbeat, and live a life full of love and connection. You deserve it."

Tears welled up in Michael's eyes, streaming down his face as he embraced Marco tightly. The hug was filled with the intensity of their shared experiences and the pain of their imminent goodbye. "I love you too, Marco. I don't know what to say... You've shown me a world I never thought I'd know, and I will always be grateful for our time together," Michael whispered, his voice choked with emotion.

Slowly, they released each other, and Marco cupped Michael's face gently in his hands. His smile was tender, yet filled with a profound sincerity. "You will always have a special place in my heart," he said, his words a promise etched into the fabric of their souls.

Marco leaned in, placing a gentle kiss on Michael's forehead. Their eyes locked one last time, filled with love and the pain of parting. They shared a long, final embrace, their bodies pressed together, hearts beating in unison.

"May we meet again in this life or another," Marco whispered, his breath warm against Michael's ear.

Marco began to step away, touching his fingers to his lips and waving Michael a kiss. "*E così va*," he said softly.

Michael nodded, unable to speak through his tears, gripping the silver coin tightly. He watched Marco walk away, the distance between them growing with each step. The camera lingered on this bittersweet moment, capturing the depth of their love and the sadness of their farewell. A single tear streamed down Michael's cheek, his heart aching with the knowledge that their paths may never cross again, but that their love and connection would remain forever.

Chapter 48

In his hotel room, Michael carefully packed his bags, each fold of clothing imbued with a newfound sense of gratitude for the experiences he'd had. The room was filled with the gentle sound of the cathedral bells chiming in the distance, their melody resonating through the Venetian air, bringing a symphony of memories to life.

Michael paused, picking up the silver coin from the dresser. He gently caressed the etched acorn, feeling the texture beneath his fingertips. Tears welled up in his eyes, a bittersweet mix of joy and sadness. Bringing the coin to his lips, he planted a soft kiss on it.

"*Grazie mille*, Marco... *Grazie mille*," he whispered, his voice heavy with emotion.

Clutching the coin close to his heart, Michael allowed himself a moment to reflect on the love and lessons Marco had given him. He took a deep breath, determined to carry these memories with him, forever cherishing the beauty of his time in *Venezia*.

Stepping out into the crisp morning air, Michael felt the city's embrace one last time. He climbed aboard his watertaxi, the gentle sway of the boat a familiar comfort. As the boat moved out into the canal and then the Venetian lagoon, the wind whipped through his hair, carrying with it a sense of liberation.

Michael felt a surge of empowerment and vitality course through him. His eyes sparkled with feeling, and his heart swelled with newfound confidence. For the first time in his life, he felt truly alive. The majestic city of *Venezia* receded behind him, its ancient beauty fading into the horizon, but the impact of its charm remained etched in his soul.

As the boat glided across the lagoon, Michael's emotions swirled within him—a mixture of hope, empowerment, and a tinge of sadness. The world around him glistened with new possibilities, and his eyes fixated on the horizon, embracing the beauty of an unknown future.

His inner warrior spirit ignited, as if fanned by the breeze sweeping across the lagoon. Michael leaned back, allowing the warmth of the sun to wrap him in its embrace. The gentle lapping of the water against the boat was a soothing soundtrack to his thoughts, each wave a reminder of the fluidity and continuity of life.

He watched as the city he had come to love slowly disappeared from view, feeling a profound sense of gratitude for the transformation he had undergone. The experiences, the connections, and the lessons learned in *Venezia* had opened his heart and mind in ways he had never imagined.

As the watertaxi sped forward, Michael felt a deep sense of readiness for whatever lay ahead. The horizon before him was a canvas of infinite possibilities, each moment an opportunity for new beginnings. He was ready to face the next chapter of his life with courage, openness, and a heart full of love.

With a final glance back at the city, Michael smiled,

feeling the weight of the silver coin in his pocket - a symbol of his journey and the growth he had experienced. As he turned his gaze forward once more, he knew that he carried *Venezia* within him, its essence a part of his very being, guiding him toward a future filled with promise and light.

The boat moved steadily across the lagoon, the sun rising higher in the sky, casting a golden glow over the water. Michael felt the warmth on his skin, a reminder of the enduring beauty of the world and the endless potential that lay within him. As he embraced the journey ahead, he knew that he was ready to live a life full of love, connection, and infinite possibilities.

ABOUT THE AUTHOR

ELLA SPENCER

With a background in literature and a passion for exploring the intricacies of human relationships, Ella's love for travel and adventure often finds its way into her novels, bringing vibrant settings to life and adding an extra layer of enchantment to her tales.

When she's not writing, Ella enjoys exploring new cultures, savoring exotic cuisines, and spending time with her beloved family. She currently resides in a charming coastal town, where she continues to dream up new stories that celebrate the beauty of love in all its forms.

More from Dikenga Books:

www.DIKENGA.com